D0961984

Spindrift and the Orchid

Also by Emma Trevayne

Flights and Chimes and Mysterious Times
The Accidental Afterlife of Thomas Marsden
The House of Months and Years

Coda
Chorus

Spindrift
and the
Orchid

EMMA TREVAYNE

Simon & Schuster Books for Young Readers

NEW YORK   LONDON   TORONTO   SYDNEY   NEW DELHI

SIMON & SCHUSTER BOOKS FOR YOUNG READERS

An imprint of Simon & Schuster Children's Publishing Division

1230 Avenue of the Americas, New York, New York 10020

SIMON & SCHUSTER BOOKS FOR YOUNG READERS

is a trademark of Simon & Schuster, Inc.

For information about special discounts for bulk purchases, please contact Simon & Schuster Special Sales at 1-866-506-1949 or business@simonandschuster.com.

The Simon & Schuster Speakers Bureau can bring authors to your live event. For more information or to book an event, contact the Simon & Schuster Speakers Bureau at 1-866-248-3049 or visit our website at www.simonspeakers.com.

Jacket design by Krista Vossen

Interior design by Hilary Zarycky

The text for this book was set in Granjon LT Std.

Manufactured in the United States of America

0418 FFG

First Edition

2 4 6 8 10 9 7 5 3 1

Library of Congress Cataloging-in-Publication Data

Names: Trevayne, Emma, author.

Title: Spindrift and the orchid / Emma Trevayne.

Description: First edition. | New York : Simon & Schuster Books for Young Readers, [2018] | Summary: After their death, Spindrift's parents leave behind one keepsake—a glass orb containing a magical orchid that has the power to make all her wishes come true, but the allure of this extraordinary orchid puts Spindrift's life in danger, leaving her to wonder whether a wish is just a curse in disguise.

Identifiers: LCCN 2017057106 (print) | LCCN 2018000683 (eBook) | ISBN 9781481462594 (hardback) | ISBN 9781481462617 (eBook)

Subjects: | CYAC: Orphans—Fiction. | Magic—Fiction. | Orchids—Fiction. | Wishes—Fiction. | BISAC: JUVENILE FICTION / Fantasy & Magic. | JUVENILE FICTION / Action & Adventure / General. | JUVENILE FICTION / Mysteries & Detective Stories.

Classification: LCC PZ7.T73264 (eBook) | LCC PZ7.T73264 Sp 2018 (print) | DDC [Fic]—dc23

LC record available at https://lccn.loc.gov/2017057106

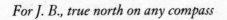

For J. B., true north on any compass

ACKNOWLEDGMENTS

The first spark of an idea for Spindrift came, as far as I can remember, out of nowhere and sat in the back of my head for quite a while. By the time I began to work on her, my own life was going through a period of adventure that, at times, mirrored Spindrift's: we took a sea voyage together, saw new places, wished for things. We had fun, maybe more than I can ever remember having with a book before, but of course, we weren't on the journey alone. The following people helped make Spindrift and her story what they are.

My eternal thanks to Jane and Tony for everything, to James for making me laugh, and to Jill for being the reason the orchids are orchids.

Thank you to Heidi, always and forever (#hashtag), and Tom for a friendship so natural and organic I think we bought it at Whole Foods. I love you both.

To my brilliant editor, Zareen: You had some almost magical sense of the freedom I needed to find this story and fall in love with writing it. Thank you for that and the million ways you made it better. My thanks as well to everyone on the S&S team, the designers, copyeditors, and marketing geniuses who shepherd a book from draft to object. Profuse thanks to Ji-Hyuk Kim for the stunning cover.

Thank you to you, the reader, for picking up this book or any other. Stories are how we change the world.

CHAPTER ONE

A Story Finally Told

IT STARTED, AS ALMOST EVERYTHING does, with a word, just like this story. *It*, you're wondering. What is *it*?

I'll tell you. I'll tell you everything, for when you have kept a secret as long as I, the only proper choice after deciding to unburden oneself is to tell all of it, from the first word to the last one. I can say right now that the last word is *rain*, but that won't do you much good without all the ones before it, so I'll share those, too, in the right order. I have stayed silent this long and could do so for whatever time I have left to me. I've stayed silent out of respect, yes, and out of fear as well, if I'm honest. The time comes, however, when one must stop being afraid.

Should someone read this and choose to seek out the mystery for themselves, the consequences of that decision are theirs alone and do not rest on my aging shoulders.

Where was I? Oh, yes. Words. Words don't frighten me anymore, though perhaps they should. There are some things about some words I must tell you before we begin.

Any dictionary worth reading will tell you that "spindrift" is a mist over an ocean, spray thrown up to the skies by a gale's crashing waves. I've seen it with my own eyes, felt its chill on my skin, slipped on it across the decks of a great and beautiful ship pitching in a storm.

But.

"Spindrift" is something else, too. Some*one* else. She is a girl, of dark hair and seawater-blue eyes and skin as pale as whitecaps. A girl who thought she was ordinary.

And the orchid is not only a precious, blooming flower. It is a curse.

—M. D.

17th day of the Month of Souls, in the Year of the Forgiven
N 48°51'24", E 2°21'03"

CHAPTER TWO

The Customer

T HE LANE WANDERED SLOWLY, TURNING this way and that as if to look in the shop windows at the work being done by the artists and artificers within, or peer through the glass of the hothouses at the rare, vivid blooms. From a distance came the sounds of the river, its waters churned by merchant ships bringing silks and spices, oysters and pearls, and of course, orchids, the latter the most prized bounty of all.

At the end of the lane, where the doorframe rotted gently and the cobblestones slipped underfoot, a shop waited for customers.

It never had to wait long, though this was not the kind of place people wandered into by accident. Its proprietor

could easily have afforded one of the large, gilded proper-
ties on Magothire Street, where even the trees were leaved
in gold and silver, but he preferred to stay where he was.
Those who needed him—and that number included a
wide swathe of the city's alchemists, inventors, nobility—
knew how to find him while maintaining their privacy.
One kept out so many undesirable customers by being
difficult to find.

The girl sitting at the shop's counter thought, personally,
that it got any number of strange customers, but her grandfather seemed to think they were the right kind of strange.

Her elbows made marks on the polished wood in front
of the book she was supposed to be reading. Instead, she
daydreamed of an ocean she couldn't quite remember,
salt and spray and fin. Like the scales of a fish, the images
flashed in and out of her mind too quickly to catch. If she
closed her eyes and tried, truly tried, she couldn't recall
anything at all. It was only when she was doing something else that the air would briefly, suddenly tinge with
the scent of seawater.

Grandfather had forgotten, in that way of his, that there
was no school today. He often forgot to put shoes on, too,
shuffling around in a pair of threadbare slippers, or to turn
on the lamps when the sky outside began to darken.

The absentmindedness didn't worry her, though,

because it came from his brain being full to bursting with other things. A customer could come in and ask for a set of clairvoyant wind chimes (which would always play the music the owner was thinking of at that particular moment) or binoculars for looking at a specific moment of the past or a book that wrote itself page by page as the reader watched. Grandfather would knit his bushy eyebrows together for an instant before unearthing the very thing from the dimmest recesses of the farthest shelf. If the shop didn't have what the customer was looking for, Grandfather would get a faraway look in his eye as he remembered exactly when he'd last sold such a thing.

Spindrift didn't know the contents of the shop nearly so well. Oh, she was good enough at the things in the cabinets that lined the walls of the front room and in the glass display cases set into the wooden counter, but she didn't understand the objects the way Grandfather did. To her, they were simply wood and metal and crystal and cloth, whereas to Grandfather they seemed almost alive.

So it was a good thing that when he left her alone to mind the shop, as he had done today, he always promised, just before he closed the door behind him, that he wouldn't be gone long. If someone came needing something complicated, she might not be able to help as well as he could.

In fact, she'd had only one customer, a grumpy old lady who complained a compass she'd purchased didn't work. It was supposed to point her in the direction of wherever she wanted to go, and yet it had taken her to her sister's home. Since they didn't speak, obviously the compass was quite broken. Spindrift suggested the woman come back to speak to Grandfather when he was here, but she was having none of it. Sighing, Spindrift opened a drawer behind the desk and traded the compass for a small pile of gold coins.

She went back to her book, which was interesting not because one of her teachers had assigned it—that could be hit or miss—but because the history of Lux, the city spread out around her, was fascinating to Spindrift since it wasn't her history. She had come here when she was young, after the accident. The sea was her home; she only lived here.

While she didn't know the shop as well as Grandfather, she knew the sound of the door creaking open as well as her own voice. Some customers barged in, certain of themselves and certain they were ready to part with a whole handful of weighty gold coins for one (or several) of the treasures here. Others tiptoed, perhaps deciding that they were here merely to look, not purchase. Invariably, however, Grandfather found something that took their fancy so thoroughly they simply had to have it, right this minute.

This customer was somewhere in the middle. He stepped inside, but kept one arm out straight and rigid to hold the door open, as if he might dart out of it again without a word. His clothing was too heavy for summer, a thick black brocade, the coat buttoned all the way to the neck.

"Good morning," said Spindrift politely. Grandfather wouldn't be pleased if he thought she'd chased anyone off with rudeness.

The man's thin eyebrows rose. They were as black as his clothing, and his hair, too. He hesitated, quite clearly waiting for someone older and more responsible to step out from behind a curtain to serve him. Not this short, thin thing of a girl, halfway through a child's schoolbook.

A chillier wind than Spindrift expected blew through the open door and rustled the book's pages. So perhaps he needed the heavy coat, after all. "May I help you?" she asked.

He tilted his head to one side, which made his long hair brush his shoulder. "Possibly," he said after a moment. "I am looking for something quite specific."

Spindrift swallowed. Exactly the kind of customer she'd been hoping not to get. Then again, perhaps his wish would be so specific that he'd know the thing he sought as soon as he laid eyes on it. "All right," she answered, marking her place in her book and hopping down from the high stool Grandfather kept at the counter for her. "What is it?"

"Well, it's . . . it's difficult to explain, you see."

This was not an unusual answer among Grandfather's clientele. "Go on," said Spindrift.

The man's hands—gloved, she noticed now—folded and writhed together. The door swung shut, but he made no attempt to inspect the cases and cabinets for his mysterious object. Instead his eyes followed every one of Spindrift's smallest movements as if she would abruptly leap over to a shelf and withdraw the thing he wanted without him having told her what it was.

"It . . . Well, it hardly matters. An unimportant trinket, I assure you. Simply a token I wanted as part of a collection."

"What sort of token?"

"A flower."

Now it was Spindrift's turn to raise her eyebrows. "A flower?" she repeated. There *were* flowers here on occasion. Elegant roses crafted in finest gleaming silver, whose thorns could be tipped with poison, or crystal lilies that would remain unchanged for years, decades, until they wilted on the day of their owner's death. Grandfather didn't have anything like that now, so far as she knew. This man would have to return when Grandfather was here.

"A black flower, one that blooms as you look at it," said the man. A strange, slow smile crept over his thin face. "Tell me, little girl, have you ever seen such a thing?"

Spindrift pictured her grandfather, the deep thought he entered as he remembered everything that had ever passed under his nose in this shop. She didn't have his memory for it, but she felt sure she'd remember something like what the man described. "No," she said, meeting the customer's eyes. "I'm sorry. I've never seen anything like that, but if it's a living flower you're after, you might try one of the hothouses. You passed a few on your way here, and there's larger ones on Magothire Street. I've seen ones that do special magic, especially the orchids. Maybe there's a kind that blooms in front of you; I know the hunters are always bringing new ones back."

The man's smile spread, reaching his obsidian eyes. "An orchid," he whispered. "Yes."

Grandfather returned a few hours later, which was an interesting interpretation of *I won't be long*, but he could be like that. Had been like that all Spindrift's life, or all of it she'd lived with him, which was nearly the same thing. There'd been no more customers after the slightly odd orchid seeker, who had left with his hands empty but his eyes still full of that strange smile. Spindrift told Grandfather about him because he always wanted to know who'd visited the shop in his absence, but he merely shrugged and took his place behind the counter, allowing Spindrift to return to her book. She was halfway through when the sun began to sink and her stomach began to rumble.

With the shop locked up tight, Spindrift and Grandfather climbed the stairs in the back to the home they shared above. Before she arrived as a baby, Grandfather had lived in just two of the rooms, a groove in the carpet worn between the one where he slept and the kitchen for his endless cups of tea. After she came, however, he had put furniture everywhere and set up a nice room for her, with a cot to keep her safe until she grew old enough for a proper bed.

She liked hearing stories about his life before she'd come to Lux, on the rare occasions she could persuade him to tell them. All too often he changed the subject to her schooling or what she might want for her birthday or when her two best friends, Max and Clémence, were next coming to dinner.

Now he went straight to the kitchen and suddenly started to move with the speed and dexterity of a man half his age. It might surprise some of his customers to learn that Ludovic Morel was one of the best chefs in all of Lux, at least as good as the cooks in the palace or the restaurants near it, where the waiters spoke in whispers and wore gloves so as not to smudge the silver spoons. Then again, perhaps it would surprise no one, given the attention he lavished on the treasures he sold. Either way, Spindrift sometimes thought chickens would line up like customers for the privilege of being roasted by him. He stood at the counter, his back to her so she couldn't see what he was creating, but she was sure it would be something delicious. Her stomach growled again, even louder, and he laughed, a dry, old laugh that matched his stooped shoulders and white hair and, somehow, his threadbare slippers too.

"Patience, *chérie*," said Grandfather. "It won't be long, and worth the wait in any case. Have you finished your book?"

"Not yet, but I will."

"Good girl. Go wash your hands and prepare the table, please."

"Will we need spoons for dessert?" she asked hopefully, and he laughed again.

"Of course, my little Spindrift. Now, hurry."

She turned from the kitchen doorway and skipped through the apartment, making her feet thump as heavily as possible on the patches of wood between the rugs. There was no one in the shop below to disturb. Her fingers trailed over the fancy silk wallpapers. The pattern of raised flowers made her think of the customer and his orchid; she hoped he'd found what he was looking for at one of the hothouses. Moonlight streamed through the large windows and painted the surrounding rooftops silvery white. If she stood at the window in her bedroom and squinted, she would just see it glinting off the glass roofs of those same hothouses, the delicate plants within them well protected.

But Grandfather had told her to hurry. Quickly she washed her hands and dried them on her skirt, ignoring the perfectly clean and usable towel hanging from a hook.

She didn't know what had possessed her grandfather to put such a large table in the dining room when she came to live here; it had been just her, not a dozen hungry sailors.

Only Spindrift had survived, blown safely back to land as if she'd been light as mist. She was sure that wasn't the way it *really* happened, but since it had probably been terrifying and she couldn't remember it anyway, it did no harm to keep a nicer picture in her head. Also, it was why Grandfather called her Spindrift instead of her actual name, and she liked that.

She knew only bits and pieces of the real story because she'd been so young, and no one else who'd been there could tell her anything now. Grandfather had put together some of it from the people who'd found her and the note tucked into her blankets, wrapped in oiled leather to protect it from the water. But these things together didn't tell the whole tale. It was like when she and Grandfather used this table to assemble puzzles; she had a corner, a few strips of edge. Only when the last piece was in place would the picture begin to move, revealing truth and memory.

Unfortunately, most of the pieces were at the bottom of an ocean, never to be found and gathered together.

The dessert spoons clattered into place. Spindrift couldn't remember having set the rest of the table, but there everything was, knives and forks and spoons and thick linen napkins. Grandfather always sat at the head of the table and she always sat to his right. The ornate chandelier above was a relic from his shop, a rare artifact that had come into his hands and with which he'd been unable to part. Right now it was the moon, with tiny stars circling around it. At daybreak it would shift, become a sun that brightened with each passing morning hour. Below it, farther down the table, was a vase of roses, their buds still tightly furled. Spindrift stared at one for several seconds, willing it to bloom as she watched.

Nothing happened. Slightly disappointed, she took goblets from a cabinet in the corner to be filled with water and elderflowers for herself, wine for Grandfather. He must have heard the clink of crystal because he appeared with a tray covered by a silver dome. It was almost always just the two of them—and when they had guests it was only Clémence and Max—yet he served dinner every night as if it were the grandest of occasions.

"Your napkin," he said as he set down the tray. Spindrift unfolded it and put it across her lap.

"Thank you. Your mother would never forgive me if she thought I wasn't teaching you your manners," he said. His eyes twinkled and his tone was light, but Spindrift sat up straighter and gave him a sharp look. He didn't often mention her mother; he would always wait until Spindrift asked and then answer her questions—or tell her as much as he thought she should hear, which often wasn't the same thing. "She was always very tidy," he continued. "Though I don't suppose there were very many clean napkins on her ship."

"Why didn't you ever visit her on it?" Spindrift asked. "Surely she would have let you."

"Begged me," said Grandfather with a smile, "but I far prefer looking at the ocean to being bounced around upon it, thank you very much. And it so rarely came anywhere near Lux. Emilie was off sailing the world with your father, and soon enough with you as well, but she wrote me a great many letters. I still have them, and it occurs to me . . ." Grandfather cleared his throat and removed the silver dome from the platter. So hungry before, Spindrift now paid no attention to the food. "Yes. I've been thinking it is perhaps time for me to share them with you."

Her stomach felt suddenly full, though she hadn't taken a bite, but full of something that wriggled and lurched. "Letters?" she asked, her mouth dry. "What sort of letters?"

"Oh, you know. News from the seas, from her adventures." He did not look at Spindrift as he said this, making a show of filling her plate and placing it before her.

"Why now?" It was a dangerous question; it might make Grandfather think twice about giving her the letters, but it was out of her mouth before she could stop it. Still, he didn't meet her eyes. Water splashed onto the table as he filled her goblet from a jug held in a shaking hand. Only when the water was at the brim did he set the jug down and raise his head.

"You are growing, little Spindrift, faster than I would like, perhaps. I am growing older, too, so perhaps it is a good thing you are turning into such a young lady, a person. And a person should know where they come from, or as much of that as is possible."

"Can we read them now?"

"After dinner, and I warn you there are more than we will get through in one evening. It will be a project for us, or if you prefer, you may read them on your own. I would understand."

"No," said Spindrift. "I don't think so. We'll do it together."

Finally, his smile returned. He patted her hand and picked up his fork. "First, food. Nothing worth doing can be done on an empty stomach. Bon appétit."

CHAPTER THREE

Messages from the Sea

12th day of the Month of Origins, in the Year of the
Wind
N 50°54'0", W 1°24'0"

Dearest Papa,
Are you quite sure you won't come and see the
Masdevallia? She is a beautiful ship, and we won't
be very far away from you before we set sail. All
right, I know you won't, and that you must think you
went wrong somewhere to cause your only daughter
to run away and marry a captain. I am happy, Papa,
and excited for this grand adventure, although to be
honest with you, I am a little bit frightened, too. The

ocean is such a vast thing, and so unforgiving when it's angry. I'd better try to make it like me so it has no reason to rage!

I must go. What seems like forty men are running around with ropes, shouting at one another, and I don't want to be seen as just the captain's wife, afraid to get her hands dirty. I'm not sure how much help I can be, but I will try.

Stay safe on dry land, and I'll see you soon.

Love,

Emilie

Spindrift's fingers traced the faded ink just as they had earlier traced the flowers on the wallpaper, the words creased by faint lines where the letter had been folded over and over again. Her mother had written this, in neat, even handwriting. A note of no importance, some might say, but Grandfather had kept it even before he knew what was going to happen. She looked at the date and counted back in her mind to the Year of the Wind, four years before she was born, fifteen years ago. And the Month of Origins . . . Spindrift's mother and father had been married in the snow and set sail on their big, gleaming ship at the start of a new year.

"Did you miss her when she left?" Spindrift asked,

still not letting go of the paper, worn thin by time . . . and Grandfather's careful rereadings?

"Of course," he said, "but she was grown, and it was time for her to make her own place in the world. She and Theo—your father—were well matched. I believed she would be happy. I think she *was* happy." His hands trembled as he reached for the letter Spindrift held. She didn't want to let it go, though there were dozens more. She wished she could read them all at once.

The chandelier overhead dimmed briefly as a cloud passed in front of the high moon. It was late, and if she dawdled any more, she might not get to read another tonight. Spindrift released the letter, and Grandfather put it back in its envelope—which, just like the letter, had clearly been folded several times so it became a small square. A small square that might fit inside something else. Spindrift smiled; she knew how the letters had been sent.

Now, however, Grandfather kept them spread flat and lined up neatly on end in a wooden box he'd fetched and placed on the table after the remains of dinner had been cleared away. The top was inlaid with enameled plants, and he'd opened the brass lock with a matching key.

He took out the second letter, and she stared at the envelope for a moment. Grandfather's name was written across the front, creased with the same old folds as the first. Inside was another short note that spoke mostly of the weather at sea. A few of the words were smudged, struck by ancient raindrops.

Although it didn't say very much, Spindrift thought these might be some of the best sorts of letters—the kind written not because the person had something important to say, but because they didn't and wanted to say it anyway. It was dated in the Month of Glass, only a few weeks after the first one.

"She was in the north," said Grandfather, pointing at the strange series of letters and numbers on the page. "I'll show you." He rose from the table, and a moment later Spindrift heard him remove a book from one of the many shelves in the parlor. An atlas, she saw when he returned, one she had occasionally used for schoolwork. "Read me those coordinates," he said. She did, and he showed her how to look up the precise spot where the ship had been, a tiny dot on the face of an enormous world. Even the ocean was frozen there, Emilie had written, and the ship had needed to carve its way through the floating sheets, the ice cracking like gunfire all around them. She would write again soon, she promised, once her hands had warmed up enough to hold a feather quill again.

And so it went. Spindrift read the next letter, and the next, looking up where they'd been sent from with Grandfather's help, but absorbing the words silently to herself. After the fifth, Grandfather fished a piece of red card from the depths of his pockets and slotted it into the box to mark their place. There were still a great many letters behind it; it seemed Emilie had written whenever she had the paper to do so.

"I think that's enough for tonight," said Grandfather. He pointed up at the chandelier, the moon almost at its highest point. Spindrift's heart sank. It was later than he usually allowed her to stay up, and though there was again no school in the morning, she would have to wake to help with breakfast and open the shop.

"Can we read more tomorrow?"

"Of course. Now, go to bed, and don't forget to wash."

Spindrift stood, then leaned down to kiss his cheek. When she left him, he was staring at the box, his hands folded on the table and head slightly bowed.

This was surely difficult for him, and yet she couldn't quite stifle a flare of irritation at how long it had taken him to show her. He'd kept the letters all this time, locked in their box so she wouldn't find them accidentally.

She took a deep breath. She could read them now; that's what mattered. Tomorrow she'd read faster, get through more than a handful of them before Grandfather sent her off to bed. Even if they all spoke of ordinary things, they were extraordinary.

Washed and in her nightclothes, Spindrift curled her bare toes on the chilled patch of wooden floor in front of her bedroom window. It was huge, with a seat just below the sill so she could sit and watch the city for as long as she liked, the thrum of daytime and quiet shadows of night.

This had been her room since she arrived at Grandfather's, but it hadn't been her mother's before that. Grandfather had once showed Spindrift the big wedding-cake house near Magothire Street, pointing up at the gilded window that had once been Emilie's.

Grandfather had turned quickly from the home and led Spindrift away with the promise of ice cream. She'd been much younger then, and such an obvious ploy had worked. Now she'd have more questions.

A draft blew in from somewhere, though her window was shut tight, and she shivered in her thin nightgown. For once, she didn't look at the buildings sloping away from the shop and down the hill toward the river. The sky was perfectly clear; whatever clouds had earlier blown across the chandelier were gone. She could see what seemed like a million stars.

Her parents would have been able to see those same stars from the middle of the ocean. They may even have used them as a map to guide their way. Spindrift knew sailors did that.

Most nights she didn't think about all of it, not in so much detail. Tonight was different. She could picture her mother sitting at a table—they must have had tables on the ship—dipping a quill into a bottle of ink, considering each word in her short notes. Then she'd slide them into envelopes and fold them up, over and over until they were tiny enough to fit into the belly of a small brass bird. Its clockwork wound up, its instructions whispered, it would soar out over the water, flying without need for rest or food, and land on Grandfather's doorstep.

A dozen such birds were this minute on a shelf in the shop below Spindrift's icy toes. Grandfather often used them to send her notes at school, to ask her to pick up milk, or apples for a tart, on her way home.

The door opened. Her stomach fluttered like wings. She was supposed to be in bed.

But her grandfather didn't seem annoyed. He came over and put his hand on her shoulder as she kneeled by the window. "It is normal to miss them more at some times than at others," he said.

"Do you?" she asked.

"Oh, yes. Sometimes, I . . . almost . . . forget. Of course, I can never truly forget, but when the shop is busy, or I am deciding whether the stew needs sage or tarragon, I don't think about it so much." He let out a deep breath.

"Then something reminds me, or I see you . . ."

"I'm sorry," she said.

"No! No, *chérie*. I thank the Seven Sages every day that you survived that terrible storm, and the Sages themselves only know how. All I am saying is that it is all right to miss them, and it is all right to think of other things. I also know it can be hard to truly miss someone if you don't know much about who they were."

Spindrift swallowed. "That's why you've decided to show me the letters now."

He opened his mouth, but no sound came out for a long moment. "I think it is time," he said finally. Then he chuckled. "I also think it is time for little girls to be in bed! The sooner you sleep, the sooner tomorrow will come."

"All right, all right," said Spindrift. Her bed was big and soft, and the second she climbed into it she let out an enormous yawn. Grandfather closed the curtains on the city beyond before coming over to kiss the top of her head.

"Good night," he said.

"Good night, Grandfather."

Yawn or not, Spindrift stayed awake after the door had closed behind him. A small dish of a watery liquid on the table beside her bed glowed with just enough faint blue light to see by—a clever invention by one of the alchemists her grandfather knew. Carefully, so as not to go tumbling to the floor, she leaned down and withdrew something from under the bed. Grandfather wasn't the only one with a wooden box, though this one was much smaller than the one he kept the letters in. Also, he knew she had it; he had given it to her when she was old enough that he'd been sure she wouldn't break what was inside.

What was inside was both ordinary and not: a crystal ball, in appearance precisely the same as countless others that had passed through Grandfather's shop.

But those worked—or if they did not, no customer returned to complain. This one had never shown the briefest second's glimpse of past or future, yet it was still Spindrift's most prized possession. For some reason, whoever had put her into the little boat in which she'd floated to shore had seen fit to tuck this in with her, even as the scream-filled storm raged around them. Maybe it was a trinket picked up in some distant port, given to her as a toy when it turned out to be useless, and her rescuer had placed it amid her blankets as a last gesture of comfort amid the chaos of the sinking ship.

That was one of the many parts of the story that never made sense to Spindrift. If someone had time to wrap her carefully in a blanket, put her in the boat with a letter to Grandfather and a little crystal ball, why hadn't they climbed in there with her? Why had they pushed her out to sea and hoped the Seven Sages would guide her safely to land?

The hinges of the box creaked slightly and the ball, sitting on a bed of green silk, caught the light from the alchemist's dish. The surface was smudged with finger-prints from all the times Spindrift had taken it out and looked at it since she'd last remembered to polish it clean. She rubbed it over the blanket on her knees, which helped a bit.

The ball would have been a large and heavy toy for a baby to hold, but it fit perfectly into her cupped hands now. She stared into it the same way she'd done almost every night for years, expecting the same nothing to hap-pen. Her eyes were heavy with exhaustion, and the orb swam in and out of focus. It had been a long day. Without even meaning to, Spindrift leaned back on her pillows. She could vaguely hear Grandfather pottering around in the kitchen, the sound of a whistling kettle and a spoon clinking against a china cup. The noises were so soothing, so ordinary. Her eyes drifted closed, and she began to sink down into the bed, but her fingers stayed curled around the crystal ball.

Unseen, it flickered.

In its depths, something black bloomed for an instant and quickly faded away.

CHAPTER FOUR

City of Light

7th day of the Month of Rains, in the Year of the Wind
N 13°6'21.6", W 59°37'55.2"

Dearest Papa,
I have been on the ocean for almost two months
now, and I never imagined I would love it as much
as I do. Theo has been teaching me all about cap-
taining the ship, and I know how to tie at least
twenty different types of knot now. Mostly we are
simply moving cargo from one place to another—
silks and spices and the like, though there've been a
few chests of things I suspect you'd like to get your
hands on for the shop. I tried to buy them, but one

of your competitors had gotten to them first. As promised, I'm looking in every port we visit, and if some particular treasure catches my eye for you, I will be sure to send it or deliver it myself if it is very valuable.

We have also had some guests aboard, though I suppose "guests" might be the wrong word. They called themselves botanists, but of course they were simple orchid hunters wanting to investigate the flowers of an island we were passing. All four of them had the fevered light of promised gold in their eyes; I hope they find the blooms that will make them rich before they starve to death. We dropped them off with their equipment and—I hope—enough food to last them until they can be fetched back again. I must say, despite the storms we are currently experiencing and the way the ship bobs around like a cork on the water, I feel much safer on the decks than I would stranded on a deserted island.

Nonetheless, I understand their quest better than they knew.

I hope things are well back in Lux. I miss you very much, and my friends of course, but with every day I am away I feel more and more like I am ful-

filling some kind of destiny. Like this is where I am supposed to be.

I suppose I do not need to explain that to you. You know what I'm looking for, and I know you're worried. Don't be, Papa. It will be different this time.

Love,

Emilie

"What was she looking for?" Spindrift asked, rereading her mother's final words several times, trying to make sense of them.

Grandfather took a long swallow of tea. "A treasure," he said, setting down his cup. It rattled in its saucer. They were sitting in the comfort of the parlor, full from a splendid supper, Spindrift curled in one corner of the velvet couch with the letter on her lap. Here and there the ink was smudged, perhaps by the rains Emilie spoke of.

"For the shop?"

"No, though she sent me many other things she found." He laughed softly. "For a time she was my best supplier, knowing exactly the sort of things I wished to see and what our customers here would buy. She was always right. A package would arrive and within a day someone would appear at the door, coins in hand, wanting that very thing. They may not have *known* they wanted it, but as soon as they saw it . . ."

Spindrift nodded. It was often like that in Grandfather's shop. "What kinds of things?"

"Oh, everything." Grandfather waved his hand. "You see, here in Lux we have our own gifts and talents, the things we're known for. Our alchemists are revered the world over, and some of our metalworkers, too. Other places are known for other things, different kinds of magic. Emilie had a . . . sense of these things. Almost as if she could smell anything unusual and wondrous. Set her down in any street, anywhere, and she would find the place where one could, for the right price, purchase a pair of feather wings to let a person fly, or a cloak that changed color depending on one's mood."

"But those weren't what she was looking for? So what was it?"

Grandfather shifted, and Spindrift's eyes narrowed. "These letters tell a story," he said. "Why don't we let them tell it? They do so far better than I can. When you read a book, do you start at the ending?"

"Of course not," said Spindrift, who sometimes did. "But I don't want to wait until the end." There were still many dozens of letters to read.

"And you won't have to. The answers will come soon, *chérie*, I promise you."

"Fine," said Spindrift, scowling slightly. "But the treasure is why she left?"

"She left because your father came in one day searching for a particular kind of telescope, and in him she saw all of her dreams coming true at once. After that she never had eyes for anyone else, and a good thing, too, for if they'd never met I wouldn't have you." Grandfather smiled. "A particularly good thing because I think she was right. She may have been worried at the beginning, or frightened of the ocean, but your mother became one of the most respected sailors ever to stand on the deck of a ship. The ocean was where she was supposed to be. How that happened, I'll never know. Her sea legs stood far sturdier than mine ever did."

Spindrift blinked. "I thought you were afraid of the ocean?" she asked. For as long as she could remember, she'd known this to be true. He often winced when he spoke of it.

"Fear is a thing that can swell like a storm," he answered. "Growing and growing. When I was young, foolish, reckless, I could almost ignore the depths beneath me. And it is a privilege of age and success that I may now send others out to stock my shelves while I remain on dry land. Fear is also a thing that can wilt like a flower under a baking sun if need for something burns hot enough, and so it was for your mother. The ocean was her home."

There it was again, a memory of a memory, the faintest wisp of salt on the breeze coming through the parlor's stained-glass windows. The sound of crashing waves in Spindrift's ears that was really just her blood thrumming through her veins.

"Another?"

"Yes, please."

He moved the piece of red card and removed the next letter, gazing at it for a moment before passing it to Spindrift. She unfolded it and began to read.

5th day of the Month of Fools, in the Year of the Wind
N 0°2'2", W 51°3'59"

Dearest Papa,
Before anything else, I must tell you to expect a package soon. No, I will not say what it is. You'll have to wait and see, but I'm sure you will love it as much as I did when I set eyes on it. To be honest, I nearly kept it for myself, but such a wonderful thing would be wasted even on the beautiful Masdevallia. *I already have a good view of the*

stars every night, and the sun shines so brightly every day now that the rains have stopped.

Spindrift looked up from the letter, wondering. Her grandfather nodded. "The chandelier," he said. "I couldn't bring myself to sell it, though there were several who tried to convince me."

She was glad he hadn't let anyone else take it.

We are in a very small port today, dropping off food supplies for those who live here. I'm not sure I've ever experienced such heat. I feel like I'm being roasted like a chicken every time I step out of the shade. Another ship is heading back east, so I will send this note and your mysterious package with its captain, who is an old friend of Theo's. He seems to know everyone everywhere. It's really quite remarkable.

Your package is something of an apology, or possibly a bribe for your forgiveness. You see, it might be a little while before you hear from me again. We are about to set off on our longest journey yet, heading almost as far south as it's possible to go. We have no plans to stop for very long on the way, and I worry the clockwork of the birds won't last such a long journey even if wound up tight.

Do not worry about the lack of letters. I will be safe, and will write again as soon as I can. And do not write. I keep each letter you send to me, and I would hate for one to get lost.

Love,

Emilie

"I still worried," said Grandfather, folding the letter away, "but she was all right, of course, and sent me quite the collection of artifacts from the excursion. Those I *did* sell. If I had kept everything she found on her travels, this apartment"—he gestured with his hands at the parlor around them—"would be filled to the ceiling, with no room for us to live in it."

Spindrift giggled, picturing herself getting ready for school with a flock of clockwork birds twittering around her head, or the mirror criticizing how she'd brushed her hair, which was black and thin and straight and resisted any attempts to braid it neatly so she never bothered.

"One more? Please?"

"No," said her grandfather. "Not tonight, my dear. You have school in the morning. You need to be well rested so that brain of yours can soak everything up. I will come and read to you while you fall asleep, if you like. A story. No more letters for now."

"Fine," said Spindrift, scowling, but Grandfather knew she didn't mean it. He didn't read to her every night anymore the way he had when she was younger. Quickly she got ready for bed and under the covers. The crystal ball was back in its box under the bed; Grandfather must have found it when he helped her tidy her room this morning. She would take it out properly after he'd finished the story and tucked her in.

The book he came in with was one of her favorites, a collection of tales about witches and fairies and dragons all bound in worn green leather. Spindrift made herself comfortable on her pillows as Grandfather settled himself on the end of the bed and began to read the first one, which wasn't the best story in the book, but the beginning always is the best place to start.

She tried to stay awake, tried very hard so she could have her usual nightly moment with her crystal ball that wasn't really a crystal ball because it didn't tell the future or the past or even terrible jokes, but once again the sounds of the familiar soothed her into sleep. Her eyelids fell shut, the pale skin of them tinged blue from the glow of the alchemist's dish.

Under the bed, inside a small wooden box and on a bed of silk, something waited.

• • •

Privately, Spindrift thought herself to be a fairly easy-going person, by and large. She ate almost everything without wrinkling her nose, liked almost all the books she read, and did what Grandfather told her . . . most of the time. She did, however, absolutely loathe the uniform she was forced to wear for school. The black wool dress was hot and itchy, and with her equally dark hair and pale skin, she always thought the dress made her look like a witch from one of the stories in the book Grandfather had been reading to her last night. Real witches didn't look like that—Spindrift knew several, and they all wore perfectly ordinary clothes, often in very bright colors—but book witches always did.

"Hurry up, *chérie*," her grandfather called from the kitchen. Spindrift hastily fastened the silver buckles on her shoes and ran out of her bedroom, her heels stomping loudly on the floor.

"I'm ready."

"Do you have your schoolbag?"

Spindrift pointed to the thing that had been sitting by the door for two days. Grandfather nodded, steam from the mug in his hands curling upward to brush his bushy eyebrows. "Come on, then," he said, leading the way down the stairs.

The shop was quiet, though it never felt empty. Perhaps

a little of Grandfather *had* rubbed off on Spindrift, for the objects did sometimes seem to her to be alive, lending a presence to the wooden shelves and glass cases that was nearly human. Grandfather walked to the door, a ring of heavy keys jingling in his hand. The lock clicked open and the wind blew in, heavy with the scents it had gathered on its way along the winding lane.

"Have a good day," he said.

"I will," said Spindrift, slipping past him out onto the cobblestones and turning to wave. He'd never been a very tall man, but he looked smaller than usual, standing there in the doorway in his faded slippers. His eyes were twinkling, though, and a smile deepened the many creases on his face.

"I'll think of something good for dinner," he said as she skipped away. She was still full from breakfast, but her tummy gave a little growl of anticipation anyway. To calm it, she took a deep breath of fresh air; she hadn't actually been outside much in the past few days, between helping Grandfather with the shop and reading the letters from her mother. Often they took a walk after they'd eaten—to help with digestion, Grandfather said—but the last two evenings had been different.

It was only this year that he'd begun to let her walk to school by herself, even though she'd known the way for ages. The shop was at the end of Nightbrick Lane, so named for the dark cobbles that shone like darkness itself after it rained. At the bottom of the hill the lane joined Argent Avenue, which ran alongside the river, with its lines of silver birch trees leading all the way up to the palace on the corner of Magothire Street. Most of the metalworkers were on the other side of Argent Avenue, facing the river, and the alchemists all had their workshops on the surrounding lanes, everyone clustered together for easy access to the water. The metalworkers needed it to cool things down and the alchemists needed it to heat things up, and they all needed it for the little boats that brought supplies and took away things to be sold elsewhere.

On the opposite bank were rows of houses and a large empty patch of green beside a soaring stone arch, the Arch of the First Sage. The book she'd been reading recently talked all about it. Seven sages had brought their wisdom and magic to Lux when it was little more than a cluster of shacks huddled together for warmth, and under their guidance it had grown to a sprawling jewel of prosperity and knowledge. Six other arches were scattered across the city, the grandest of all the grand structures, in their way.

As much as she missed an ocean she scarcely remembered, it was difficult to imagine a better city than Lux.

Light, it meant, and it truly was a place that glowed every hour of the day. By sunlight the white stone buildings gleamed and the water shone a sparkling blue. The green-tinted glass of the numerous hothouses were like brand-new buds in spring. At sunset, the red and gold glow would touch on every gilded railing and silver leaf, turning them to a million tiny candle flames. And at nightfall, men in carts would travel up and down the streets, touching long, burning sticks to the gas lamps. In windows, alchemists' lamps of every color flickered.

Today the light came with a touch of brittle, crystalline chill; it might have been a good idea to bring a cloak. The wind had been a bit sheltered on Nightbrick Lane, warmed by the huddle of buildings. Coming straight off the river here, it was much cooler, and blew Spindrift's feet into a near run. She was panting—and warm—by the time she reached the palace, where she turned and crossed the long bridge, the water loud beneath her feet. Even at this hour Magothire Street was nearly full of people on their way to somewhere or from somewhere, or simply wanting to look in the windows of the enormous shops and hothouses filled with orchids that might cost more than a month's wages. Or a year's. Spindrift ducked and weaved between the people— sometimes there were advantages to being small—raced under trees leaved in gold and silver, and nearly fell through a wrought-iron gate into a somewhat quieter courtyard. Gray stone surrounded her on three sides, creating a cauldron of noise at this hour of the morning as the courtyard filled with students, all in itchy black wool uniforms like Spindrift's.

One in particular caught sight of her. Spindrift's stomach sank as he left his little knot of friends and sauntered over, polished shoes gleaming. She forced herself to look up at his face, the hard line of his chin and cruelly sneering mouth widening into something someone might call a smile, though they'd be wrong.

"Good morning, little orphan girl," he said.

"Good morning, Tristan," she said through gritted teeth. He had hated her for seemingly no reason since their first day of school, and it hadn't taken long before she'd hated him right back. Once, when she'd returned home with a skinned knee after he'd tripped her, Grandfather had told her that it happened sometimes, people simply disliking each other like that. Still, Grandfather had marched down to the school the next day, and ever since Tristan had taunted Spindrift with words and not his stupidly oversized feet.

"I was just thinking what a pleasant day it is," said Tristan, casting his eyes about at the patches of dappled sunlight before fixing them back on Spindrift.

"I suppose," she said.

"I'm so glad it's not raining."

Spindrift had no response to this. What was he blathering about?

"You must be too," he said, his not-smile stretching further. "Your family doesn't do well in storms, does it? A little bit of rain and their ship tipped right over."

The backs of Spindrift's eyes burned. "It was a terrible storm," she said, tears threatening to spill out onto her cheeks. "They did everything they could. They're perfect."

"*Were* perfect."

"Leave her alone," said a voice, and Spindrift spun around, a tear breaking free from sheer relief. Clémence reached her in a second, teeth bared. "Why must you be so awful?"

"Awful?" Tristan repeated. "We were only speaking of the weather."

"Let's go, Spin," said Clémence, taking Spindrift's arm and leading her over to Max, Clémence's twin brother and Spindrift's other best friend. They looked as alike as was possible, with the same eyes, the same dark hair and skin, but Spindrift privately thought Clémence had stolen most of the voice that should have been divided between the two of them. Clémence was loud, whereas Max spent words as if they were gold coins. "I hate him," said Clémence almost cheerfully when Tristan was out of earshot. "Are you all right?"

Spindrift nodded. She was now. Max patted her shoulder.

"Good. We have something to tell you," said Clémence, hooking her arm through Spindrift's. "We went to work with Papa yesterday and saw the drawings for the new tower. We'll be able to see the whole city from the top when it's finished!"

Everyone who lived in Lux had been talking of little but the tower for some time now, ever since it had been announced. A site had been chosen for it beside the river and the design was being kept famously secret. It was no wonder Clémence was boasting.

"What does it look like?" Spindrift asked.

The headmistress came out of the school's tall, thick wooden doors, a heavy brass bell in one of her sinewy hands poised to bring her pupils to order if her voice wasn't enough. Madame Dulac wasn't a mean woman, but she was very strict.

"I'll tell you later," whispered Clémence as they filed into lines.

"I have something to tell you, too," said Spindrift.

"Silence!" said Madame Dulac. Spindrift shut her mouth and filed into the school, thinking of her mother's letters.

CHAPTER FIVE

Letters, Towers, and Lemon Tarts

THE PLOT OF LAND WHERE the tower would be was just a field of grass now, bordered on one side by the Arch of the First Sage, on two others by houses, and the fourth by the river. Without properly being able to picture the tower the way Clémence and Max, who had seen the drawings, could, it was boring. She turned her attention to the water, as she always did whenever she could see it, often without even meaning to.

The view of the city *would* be remarkable from the viewing platform set to be built at the top of the tower, high in the sky above her. From it she might be able to see the speck that was her home and Grandfather's shop, whereas from the ground she could only vaguely point in its direction on the other side of the river, across one of the many bridges that spanned the water at intervals, knitting the city together. Beyond the silver trees of Argent Avenue, Nightbrick Avenue ended halfway up a hill; from the top rose the highest of the seven arches, another confection of stone and iron.

"Here's where the four legs will be," shouted Clémence, walking in a big square. "And it will meet at a point like this," she finished, joining Spindrift and Max again and demonstrating with her hands.

"When do they think it'll be finished?" asked Spindrift, trying to be interested even though she had a hard time imagining it.

"Oh, not for two or three years at least. It'll take the alchemists that long to make all the steel for it."

Spindrift nodded. That made sense. A slightly queasy feeling overtook her stomach as she thought of standing at the top of the tower, trusting the alchemists had done their jobs properly and the metal was strong enough to stay up.

Perhaps that was how her mother had felt the first time she'd boarded the *Masdevallia*, or the first time it had been in a storm, afraid the wood would blow apart underfoot.

"Grandfather's letting me read some letters," Spindrift said, so softly that at first she wasn't sure Clémence and Max heard her. But Max missed little, and he touched his sister's arm to draw her attention back from the sky.

"Letters?" he asked.

"From my mother."

Clémence's eyes widened. "Your mother? Truly? Oh, Spin! What do they say?"

"Not much yet," Spindrift admitted, hoping they would see it was the *fact* of the letters that was important, not so much their messages. "I've only seen a few so far, about her early days on the ship. It was called the *Masdevallia*, and it was beautiful."

Max tilted his head to one side. "Were they orchid hunters?"

"No," said Spindrift. "What makes you say that?" It was true that Lux, as well as other cities beyond, had been in the grip of an orchid frenzy for decades, and her mother had mentioned orchid hunters, but why would she, if she were one herself? Besides, it was clear she'd been looking for different treasures.

"*Masdevallia* is a type of orchid," said Max, shrugging.

"Oh." Spindrift hadn't known that. Perhaps her father had bought his ship from a failed orchid hunter and never renamed it. "Well, no. But she was looking for something."

"What?" Clémence asked eagerly.

"I don't know," said Spindrift, and Clémence's face fell.

"Grandfather said the letters tell a story, and I haven't gotten to that part yet."

"You must tell us when you do! I'll bet she was looking for a pile of gold and jewels, or the answer to some ancient mystery. That's always what pirates are looking for in books."

"My mother was not a pirate!" said Spindrift, *reasonably* sure that was true.

Something flashed in the air, drawing all their attention. Something tiny and golden, catching the sun as it flew toward them. In the glare of the light, Spindrift could only just make out its fluttering wings, which slowed when it neared, coming to a stop a few inches in front of her nose.

The folded-up note inside was from Grandfather, of course, but Spindrift took longer than usual smoothing it out, thinking of her mother's letters.

3rd day of the Month of Illumination, in the Year of the Ancients
N 48°51'24", E 2°21'03"

Chérie,
Come home for supper. Bring Clémence and Max if you like.
Love,
Grandfather

Clémence and Max lived on this side of the river, but Max said, "I'll cross over if Monsieur Morel is cooking," which he surely was. The three of them found the closest bridge and walked swiftly to the other side, where it joined Argent Avenue. A few moments later they were at the mouth of Nightbrick Lane, walking up and into the arms of a commotion. Joyful shouts streamed down the cobblestones like water spilled from a bucket. They ran, following the twists and turns, until a large cart, drawn by an even larger brown horse, came into view outside one of the small hothouses. Several people, all smudged with soil, were removing large wooden crates from the cart, holding them as gingerly as if they were made of glass.

"Careful," said a woman who had often waved to Spindrift in the street; Spindrift recognized her from the curly red hair that was now tied up in a knot on the top of the woman's head.

"You don't think I know that?" asked the man on the other end of the crate. "This one was the hardest for me to get. I'll tell you the story, but you'd best sit down for it."

Ah, orchid hunters. That explained it. The craze for the flowers had been part of the fabric of the city since before Spindrift had come to live here, and she had to admit they *were* beautiful. Grandfather had bought her one once, but neither of them was particularly good with plants and she hadn't done very well at keeping it alive.

For those who were good at keeping them alive, however, there was a passion as keen as Grandfather's for the objects in his shop. The hunters traveled across the world looking for new and rare kinds, fantastical colors, ones that would bloom often or even in the coldest of winters. The rarest ones could sell for more than all the buildings on Magothire Street combined.

"Come on," said Max, whose mouth was always happier eating than speaking. Spindrift grabbed Clémence, and the three of them continued on their way. The orchid hunters' happiness made Spindrift smile to herself; she wondered if her mother felt something akin to that when she found the chandelier or some other intriguing artifact.

Or when—if—she'd found the mysterious treasure she'd been seeking. Suddenly, Spindrift was almost sorry she'd brought Clémence and Max back with her. She didn't want to read the letters with them, not the first time at least, and she wanted to know what her mother had been searching for, and whether she'd found it. Hopefully she had. Spindrift liked the idea of her mother's eyes lighting up with the thrill of finding the perfect rare thing.

In the near-hush of the shop, Grandfather was helping a customer at the counter, the two peering down at
something beneath one of the glass panels. He looked
up and smiled widely, both at Spindrift and at Max and
Clémence, who waved in response. Grandfather begged a
moment from his customers and plucked another one of
the tiny birds from the shelf behind the counter. "To let
your parents know where you are," he said to Clémence
and Max. "I'll join you shortly."

Spindrift knew the intensity in the air, and that some
very valuable things were kept in the cases; Grandfather
was about to sell something quite precious, and it was best
to leave them to it. The three of them climbed the stairs to
the apartment, and she ushered her friends into the parlor. "I'll be right back," she promised. In her bedroom,
she tore off the hated, itchy wool dress and replaced it
with a much softer one.

That was better.

She kicked her shoes under her bed and the wooden
box caught her eye. Almost every night she took out the
ball within just to look at it, but last night she'd fallen
asleep before having a chance.

Daylight still came in through the window, making
her smudged fingerprints all the more obvious on the
smooth crystal. It magnified her hand so her fingertips

looked like those of a giant, every whorl and ridge visible.

She stared at them for so long they began to shift and wriggle in and out of focus.

She blinked. Once, and again.

Something black had flashed in the center of the orb, or was it just her eyes playing tricks on her? She rubbed them with her free hand and stared again, trying to replicate what she'd done before. Following this line of her fingerprint, then that one.

Nothing happened.

Spindrift took a deep breath and concentrated as hard as she could. Something had appeared deep within the glass. She was sure of it. If she'd made it happen once, she could do it again. It was simply a matter of trying hard enough.

She stared and stared.

There! Again! Like a droplet of ink splashed into water, a midnight wisp that curled and vanished. She gripped the ball so hard her knuckles ached, but she could not let go. "Show me," she whispered, not meaning to speak aloud. "Please."

The lines on the palm of her hand stretched across the bottom of the orb and ended abruptly at the curve of the glass. Spindrift didn't move an inch, afraid to break the spell, the particular balance that had allowed . . . whatever it was . . . to happen. Her eyes began to water from strain, but she did not dare blink now; she might miss it.

An inky swirl, larger this time. *Yes.* She waited, watching its first efforts to form into . . .

A knock rang through the room. "Spin?" came Clémence's voice. "What are you doing in there? Come play a game."

The ball fell from Spindrift's hands onto the bedcovers, empty as it had been for years. "Yes," she said softly, her mouth dry, heart pulsing with frustration. "Yes, I'm coming."

Stuffed full of lamb stew and a lemon tart covered in a cloud of meringue, Spindrift began to think maybe she'd imagined something happening in the center of the crystal ball. It could have just caught the black cloth of her discarded school dress, distorting it, making it look like a drop of ink in the middle.

No, she hadn't. She knew she hadn't. She'd just eaten herself silly so that Grandfather, Clémence, and Max wouldn't suspect anything strange was going on, and now her brain was all fuzzy around the edges.

At the other end of the velvet couch, Clémence groaned, holding her stomach. Grandfather chuckled from his armchair.

"Now, now," he said. "I know for certain your parents feed you. Are they well?"

"Very well," said Clémence through a yawn. "Busy with the tower."

"Of course, of course. What a magnificent thing it will be," said Grandfather. "I may pay them a visit soon. I'm sure you haven't forgotten that your school holidays are fast approaching, and I wonder what with one thing and another whether they will be too busy to take the two of you away. If that is the case, I'm sure Spindrift and I would be delighted to have you join us on ours if your mother and father agree."

Despite her aching belly, Spindrift sat bolt upright. She had forgotten about the holidays, and this was certainly the first time Grandfather had mentioned taking a trip somewhere. "Really?" she asked, her voice filling the room. "Where are we going?"

"Yes, where?" Clémence chimed in. Max, from his place sprawled on the embroidered rug, turned his head to them, listening intently.

"I feel it is time for you to see more of the world," said Grandfather, directing his words to Spindrift. "It's a big world, and if we don't get you started soon, you might never see all of it! For this first trip we won't go too far, especially if I have three of you to keep sight of. We'll decide where after I've spoken to Max and Clémence's parents."

All other thoughts fled from Spindrift's mind. They were going on an adventure! But where? How would they get there? What would they do in some strange, thrilling place?

"For the moment it is time to see these two home safely. Max, Clémence, would you like to walk, or do you think you aren't too full for the wings?"

"Wings!" Max and Clémence chimed together. Grandfather chuckled again.

"As I suspected. All right. Get your things and come downstairs."

A few minutes later Clémence and Max stood in the middle of the shop, pairs of feathered wings on leather frames strapped to their backs. Max's were of a deep, peacock blue, Clémence's a fiery red. "Return them to Spindrift tomorrow," he said, adjusting a buckle at Max's shoulder so it held more tightly. The twins nodded. They'd done this before. "And be careful."

"Yes, Monsieur Morel. Thank you for dinner."

"My pleasure. Now, home, and no dawdling on the way."

"Bye, Spin!" said Clémence. "See you at school."

"Good night," said Spindrift, wishing she could fly with them for the fun of it, but there was no good reason to. And then she remembered the letters, and the crystal ball that maybe-definitely had shown a drop of ink in its center, and was glad they were leaving. Shame heated her face, and she turned toward the stairs as Max and Clémence squeezed their way through the shop door, feathers brushing the wooden doorframe.

She was upstairs before Grandfather had turned the lights back out, sitting at her place on the couch in the parlor, the wooden box beside her. He'd left it on a shelf below the low table the previous evening, but she couldn't open it. Grandfather's slow footsteps creaked up the stairs. Slower than usual. Perhaps he was tired.

"Why are you keeping them locked up now that I know about them?" she asked the instant his shadow crossed the parlor door. The rest of him came into view, wild-haired, skin lined with years.

"Because they are mine," he said gently. It was a simple reason, almost too simple. "I think you should see them, read them, know as much as you can about who your mother and father were, but they are nonetheless the last I have of my daughter. I would not like tea spilled on them when I wasn't looking. Or when I was looking, for that matter."

Spindrift rarely spilled tea on things. However, she didn't think arguing with him would change his mind. She was much too full to argue, anyway. And while she desperately wanted to go to her room and see if the crystal ball would do anything else, it was still early enough that Grandfather would wonder why she'd taken herself to bed, whether something was wrong. A large clock hung on the wall, its gears and mechanisms exposed so that one could see every turn of the wheel of time.

Something *was* wrong. All these years the crystal ball had sat under her bed, protected in its box. Ever since she could remember, she'd taken it out almost every day and looked at it, held it, wishing for something to happen, though she didn't know what. Today, finally, something had almost happened, and instead of delving deeper into its mysteries, she was sitting here wondering if it were actually possible to die from eating too much lemon tart.

A few of the letters, then. That would allow her stomach to settle and buy enough time to prevent Grandfather from being suspicious at her willingness to sleep.

23rd day of the Month of Illumination, in the Year of the Wind
S 51°38'0", W 69°13'0"

Dearest Papa,
See? I told you I would be all right, and that I'd write again. I am sorry it's been so long, though I

did warn you. Still, it was longer than any of us thought, and for good reason! I wonder how to encompass everything we experienced these few months in a simple letter, and whether I have enough paper to do the stories justice. I'll have to do my best, but first, is all well there? I know it is difficult for you to answer me as you don't know where to send the replies. Just know that I am thinking of you—have been thinking of you—and hoping things are good at home. Please don't spend all of your time behind the shop counter; fresh air is good for you.

And so to begin. When I last wrote, we were about to head south, which was indeed what we did at sunrise the next morning. Unfortunately, we did not get far before one of the crewmen took ill, and there was a very frightening few days when we did not know whether the rest of us might be stricken with the same malady. Luckily, the rest of us escaped whatever it was, but we were forced to make an unplanned stop in a new port to find a doctor. The locals were extremely wary of us, and I must say I can't blame them. A mysteriously ill sailor turning up unannounced is never a welcome guest, I can assure you.

To this day I have no idea what the medication contained, as I speak no words of the tongue in which it was explained to us, but whatever it was did the trick. Our crewman healed, and we set off again, behind schedule and battling a wind determined to delay us further. Theo barely slept a wink, and I helped where I could, all of us taking turns at the wheel so we could sail through the nights.

Eventually we caught up to ourselves—that is, where we should have been—and our journey continued. In the clearest hours I saw land on the horizon, but we did not stop. Our destination was far ahead, and with enough provisions in the galley to keep us fed, we did not linger.

It was the longest I have spent at sea without setting foot on solid ground, and I don't mind telling you that when I finally did, it took some time before my sea legs turned back into land legs. I wobbled all over the place, much to the amusement of Theo and the others. It was worth it, however, for our destination. A bright and colorful port in a city of equal wonder. Once again, I did not speak the tongue, but curiously, I felt as if I didn't need to. Everything that needed to be said, by me at least, could be done with a smile or my eyes. Theo had

a more difficult time of it, as of course the nego-
tiations fell to him, and it took nearly a week to
gain the trust of those he needed to speak to. He
managed in the end, and we took on an enormous
cargo of rarities whose value, when we return, will
make us richer than the king or the Seven Sages
themselves.

Or it would have done.

Grandfather, who had been reading over Spindrift's shoulder, abruptly snatched the several sheets of paper from her fingers. Sensing her shock, he patted her knee. "I'm sorry, *chérie*. Very sorry. It is just that I have remembered what the rest of this letter says, and I worry it will frighten you."

"Why? What happened?" Spindrift folded her arms across her chest. She was not so easily frightened as he seemed to think.

"Perhaps if I tell you a bit beforehand, then you will be prepared, hmmm? All right. Your mother and father did not return with a king's ransom in spices. They were . . . How do I put this . . . ? *Waylaid* on their journey back. Someone else, you see, decided that they very much wanted the *Masdevallia*'s precious cargo."

"You mean pirates?" Spindrift asked. Her grandfather

let out a sigh, apparently of relief that he didn't need to explain it to her.

"Yes, precisely. Pirates. Are you sure you wish to read it?"

Spindrift took the letter back, but her eyes could only skim over the remainder of the pages. The *Masdevallia* had been attacked by the large crew of another ship. There had been swords and screams and cannon fire, and when all was said and done, barely half of the *Masdevallia*'s crew were still standing, the holds of the ship empty of the fortune they'd just held.

Her parents had survived, of course, where so many of the others hadn't. She felt both glad and sad at the same time, and then the sadness doubled when she remembered her parents hadn't escaped danger every time.

That had been a storm, though. There wasn't anything they could have done to stop it.

"I think," said Spindrift, folding the letter up, "I don't want to read any more tonight."

"Oh, *chérie*. I am not surprised. I should have remembered and prepared you better. Would you like anything? A hot chocolate with cream?"

She was still impossibly full, and almost without her realizing it, the perfect excuse had presented itself. "No, thank you. I think I'll just go to bed, if that's all right."

"You won't have nightmares?" Grandfather's bushy eyebrows knitted together in concern.

"I won't. I promise." She kissed his cheek. "Good night."

"Good night, my dear."

As quickly as she could and as loudly as she could, she washed and got ready for bed, making a point to shut the door so that Grandfather could hear it. Yes, she was disturbed by the letter, but her parents *had* survived that time, and only a fool would think theirs had been a particularly safe choice of job. Emilie had lived to write many more letters, so Spindrift didn't need to worry about the pirates tonight.

The crystal ball was heavy and smooth in her hands, slightly cold. The night gathered itself around her in her room, illuminated only by the glow of the alchemist's dish.

She concentrated, tried to remember everything she'd done last time.

She waited, holding her breath.

The drop of black ink came, such a relief that Spindrift felt as if it had spilled from something breaking open inside her. It grew as she exhaled, swirling and forming and . . . blooming.

Blooming into the unmistakable shape of an orchid flower.

CHAPTER SIX

Black Orchid Blooming

I T WAS ALL THERE, THE petals and lip and throat. It grew and grew until it pressed against the walls of the crystal ball, and then somehow it was outside of them, stretching in midair before Spindrift's astonished gaze. It moved like silk blowing on the wind as the petals became limbs, a body, a woman's head, a mass of hair as black as a crow's wing. Her dress continued to swirl around her even as she stilled, midnight eyes staring from a pale face directly down at Spindrift.

Frozen with fear, Spindrift stared back. Nothing in Grandfather's shop had ever done anything like this. The comforting thought—that the shop was still downstairs, that Grandfather was still somewhere out in the apartment—

released her muscles, and she jumped off the bed, past the woman, and pressed herself to the wall. All Spindrift had to do was scream.

"Don't scream," said the woman. Her voice was like music, what music would sound like if each note were as perfect as a flower. "I am not here to harm you."

"What are you?" Spindrift asked, a hoarse whisper. She hoped she wouldn't have to scream; she wasn't certain now that she could. "Who are you?"

"You look frightened, child. Are you afraid?"

Yes, thought Spindrift. "No," she said, trying to uncurl her hands from the fists they'd formed. Her neck hurt; the orchid-woman was very tall. It was difficult for Spindrift to look at all of her at once.

"I think that is a lie, but I would probably tell the same one. Don't be afraid, child. As I said, I am not here to harm you. I'm here to help you. Tell me, what is your name?"

"They . . . they call me Spindrift." The woman's dress was still shifting, blowing as if in a strong breeze, though there was none. It was beautiful, mesmerizing. Somewhere, deep in the back of her mind, Spindrift thought she should shout for Grandfather, and yet she believed that the woman wasn't going to hurt her, even if she couldn't say *why* she believed it. The woman's red-lipped smile was so wide and her dark eyes so sparkly.

"Spindrift," said the woman, making it sound like a song. "That's pretty. Where am I?"

"L-Lux," said Spindrift. "This is my grandfather's house. His name is Ludovic Morel."

"Ah," said the woman. "Good. Very good."

"What did you mean, you're here to help me?"

"Exactly what I said. I'm here to give you whatever you want. Well, *almost* whatever you want. There are a few things I'm sadly unable to do." The woman appeared to sense Spindrift's confusion. "Oh, explaining's always the trickiest part when I first appear. Come, sit down. You'll be more comfortable." She patted Spindrift's bed.

Slowly, but unable to disobey, Spindrift inched over to the bed and let herself perch on the edge. "Please tell me what you are."

"It might be easier to show you. That's usually the case," said the woman, casting her dark eyes around the room. "Aha."

Spindrift startled. One second the woman had been beside her. The next she was by the window, reaching for a book on the window seat. The book of stories Grandfather had read from last night. She stroked the cover, but did not pick it up. "Brown is such an ugly color," she said. "Tell me, what color do you wish it were?"

"Blue," said Spindrift without thinking. The color of oceans.

The book turned blue.

Spindrift stood up. "How did you do that?" she demanded.

The orchid-woman held her finger to her lips. A bubble of anger inflated inside her, quickly pierced by a whistling kettle and then Grandfather's slippered feet shuffling down the corridor.

"The *how* isn't as important as the *why*," came the answer when all was silent again beyond the door. "I did it because you wished it."

The words slotted into place in Spindrift's brain. "You can grant wishes?"

"It's what I'm for," she said.

The empty crystal ball was still on the bed a few inches from Spindrift's hand. How had a thing that fit into her palm held this kind of secret? But that was a silly question. Nearly every object in Grandfather's shop had power far beyond its size, and the simplest appearance could hide the most extraordinary gift. It was all too easy to believe that a black orchid could bloom inside the crystal ball and that the orchid could then turn into a wish-granting woman, but that didn't mean Spindrift didn't have questions. Lots of them. They filled her head until she wasn't sure which one to ask first, which one was the most important. How much time would she have to ask them? Would the orchid disappear again and never come back? How many wishes was Spindrift allowed to make?

"Do you have a name?" Spindrift asked.

The woman folded her long-fingered hands together. "A name? No, not anymore, not in the same way you have a name."

Spindrift's eyes narrowed. "Not anymore?" she asked.

"I was a person once, a person of flesh and blood like yourself. Now I am . . . this."

This raised even more questions. At this rate Spindrift wasn't going to have time to wish for anything. "What was your name when you were a person?"

"Eleanor," said the woman. The name tickled something at the back of Spindrift's memory, but the feeling went almost as soon as it came. "However, if you need me so that you can make a wish, simply say *Orchid* and I will bloom."

"But . . ." Spindrift tilted her head, which for some reason made it easier to think. "But I didn't say that the first time."

"The first time is always different. I don't quite know how it happens," said Orchid. "I am nowhere, I am nothing, and then suddenly I am somewhere, and a rather surprised person is holding my crystal ball. Then I have to explain what I am and the wishes begin."

So, Spindrift wasn't the first to have the orchid; there had been others before her. This was going to take some deeper thought when the orchid wasn't standing before her, her dress of air and midnight was not swirling distractingly, and her eyes were not full of waiting. The jumbled questions in Spindrift's mind pushed and pulled at one another, each one trying to be the next to escape Spindrift's lips. "What should I wish for?"

Orchid unfolded her hands and spread her arms as wide as she could. The dress rippled. "I cannot decide for you, but there are rules, limitations. I am the black orchid. I can only affect objects. Turning your book blue was as simple as blinking. Turning *you* blue is impossible for me."

Spindrift giggled, slightly disappointed. Seeing herself blue in a looking glass would be funny, so long as she could wish herself back again before anybody saw her. Especially Tristan. She could only imagine what mean thing he'd say at such a sight.

Her smile faded. He liked teasing her about her parents, and they were what she'd most want to wish for, weren't they? But her parents were not objects. They were bones at the bottom of the ocean, and she couldn't wish them back together.

There wasn't anything else she really wanted.

"I imagine this has come as a bit of a shock," said Orchid. "It usually does. It's been very nice for me to stretch, but why don't I go back into my ball for a while so you can start thinking of wishes. You can have as many as you like, though if I may, I will offer you a warning."

"All right," said Spindrift.

"You do not seem a foolish girl. Consider, please, how valuable I am and how many other people might like to possess me. The more obvious you make your wishes, the greater the chance someone will try to take me from you."

Spindrift's head was so full she hadn't even thought of that. She desperately needed time to think. The ball was still a few inches away. Her fingers closed around it and she held it up, uncertain what to do next. Was there something she needed to say to send Orchid back inside?

Apparently not. Faster than she'd bloomed, Orchid was gone from beside the window and the crystal was full of swirling black. She watched it shrink to nothing. There wasn't the faintest hint of inky black now inside the glass.

"Orchid!" she said.

The blooming was faster this time.

"Yes?"

"I was . . . just testing."

Orchid's laugh was as musical as her voice. "Good night, Spindrift," she said, and was gone again, back into the ball.

So, it worked. The object in Spindrift's hands was more valuable than any in Grandfather's shop. More valuable than all of them put together, most likely. She wasn't stupid. She understood Orchid's warning about people who would be eager to get their hands on it.

The thought poked through all the others like a thorn piercing skin. *Why are there suddenly orchids everywhere?* All right, there were always orchids in the hothouses and the word was always on the lips of the hunters who returned with them, but this was . . . more. The *Masdevallia*, her parents' ship, named for an orchid.

The strange man in the shop when Grandfather had left her alone to mind it, he'd been looking for a black orchid that bloomed when you looked at it.

He'd been looking for this, and somehow he'd known to ask Spindrift. It was only by chance, luck, that Orchid hadn't revealed herself until after. If it had been before, Spindrift wasn't sure she would have been able to lie well enough to keep her secret. She had to hope he'd given up and wouldn't return.

There were other dangers, as close by as just the other side of her bedroom door. Spindrift loved Grandfather more than anything, but if she told him about Orchid or he noticed anything strange, he'd surely take it from her. Not out of cruelty. It was simply who he was. He'd want to know everything about it, test it, examine its magic.

It was hers and hers alone. She had to keep it to herself. Someone had put it in the little boat with her when they'd saved her life; someone had wanted her to have it.

The sun was barely touching the cobbles of Nightbrick Lane when Spindrift awoke, memories rushing back as fast as the nearby river. By the light of dawn, with birds beginning to sing in their trees, it didn't seem real. She rolled over and searched beneath the bed, fingers clutching at air until they bumped against the corner of the wooden box.

"Orchid," she said the moment she had the ball in her hands. Black ink swirled, and the flower bloomed.

"Oh," said Orchid, turning her dark eyes to the window. "Is it morning? I'm not very good with times of day, I'm afraid."

"Yes," said Spindrift sleepily. "It's morning." Part of her wished it wasn't, but she had the whole day ahead of her now to wish for things—carefully, of course. She hadn't forgotten that she needed to keep this a secret. Last night she'd thought there wasn't anything she wanted if she couldn't have her mother and father back. After a good night's sleep, the world seemed full of possibilities.

"I wish this weren't so itchy," she said, pulling on her school dress. And suddenly it wasn't. She pulled the collar free to stare at it. It looked the same as ever, no difference anyone would notice. It felt like the softest silk, cool and smooth against her skin.

"I wish this sock didn't have a hole in it." Grandfather was good at a great many things, and he took very good care of Spindrift, but some things he just didn't notice.

The sock fixed itself so perfectly the seamstress just down Nightbrick Lane wouldn't have been able to spot the mend.

"I wish my hair would behave itself," she said, inspecting it in the mirror, uncombed, sticking out in all directions like Grandfather's did.

Nothing happened. Oh. Of course. Sighing, she resolved to fix it herself, but she did wish her comb from the dresser into her hand.

This was *fun*.

Orchid made no comment on Spindrift's wishes, though Spindrift was sure she must usually get asked for more exciting things. Spindrift was just warming up. It was amazing all the things she could think of to wish for all of a sudden. She wished the buckles on her shoes were polished to a shine and (when Grandfather was safely out of the dining room) that her croissant was filled with chocolate.

For the first time in her life, Spindrift put the crystal ball in her schoolbag, heavy in the bottom under her books and pencils. It felt safer now to have it with her always, and what if she wanted to wish for something on the way?

Orchid must be able to hear her from within the crystal, or she wouldn't know when Spindrift summoned her. That only made sense. "Are you alive?" Spindrift asked. "Or are you an object?"

There was a pause long enough that Spindrift wondered if the orchid had heard her; maybe inside her ball she couldn't hear anything except the word to summon her.

But . . . "I suppose I am both, and neither. One would think that since I cannot die, I must not be alive, and yet I *can* think, which an object cannot. My ball is an object. Did you have a wish?"

"I wish you could grant wishes from inside the crystal," whispered Spindrift, and Orchid's musical laugh rang out.

"Clever. Yes, I can do this."

"Are you coming, *chérie*?" Grandfather called. Spindrift hurriedly joined him at the top of the stairs and followed him down, waiting behind him while he unlocked the door. She kissed his cheek and wished him a good day.

That was a different kind of wish. She'd been wrong the previous night; there were a great many things she wanted.

She wished the cobblestones weren't so slippery with dew and that the wind off the river wasn't quite so chilly. Instantly, the ground underfoot was dry and a warm scarf appeared about her neck. So, the orchid couldn't control the wind itself. That made sense.

She wished for an apple, and for her schoolbag to be less heavy, and that Clémence and Max would be the first people she'd see in the courtyard.

"I cannot do that," said the voice from her bag, nearly swallowed by all the other noise from crowded Magothire Street. "I cannot control others. Who are Clémence and Max?"

"My friends," said Spindrift, reaching the wrought-iron gate. She ducked inside and looked around, searching for them in the walled courtyard. She caught Tristan's eye, but thankfully the headmistress was already on the steps, her bell in her hand, and he wasn't foolish enough to be mean to Spindrift right under her long nose. Where were Max and Clémence? And how had Spindrift almost managed to be late when she'd been awake so early?

Well, all right, the walk had taken longer than it did most days, what with all the stopping to wish for things. She'd have to remember that, and be careful. It was important not to let anything seem out of place. No one could notice anything different. Orchid was *hers*.

Clémence and Max ran through the gate. "We're here!" Clémence said, breathless. "*Max* forgot the wings and we had to go back. It was freezing when we flew home. You wouldn't think it was almost summer."

Slightly behind his sister's shoulder, Max rolled his eyes and Spindrift fought back a smile. They both knew he wasn't the one who'd forgotten, though he was the one carrying them, folded up small in a heavy bag on one arm, which made him a little lopsided. Spindrift reached out and took it from him. She'd wish it lighter on the way home, but she couldn't do that here in front of Clémence and Max.

She hadn't decided yet whether she was going to tell them. Sometimes secrets were easier to keep when you shared them with just a few people, if they were the right people.

Maybe she would tell them later. The secret could be only hers for a little while longer. There was no reason to let them in on it now, after all.

The bell began to ring, the headmistress swinging it in

a wide arc, each peal bouncing loudly off the high gray stone walls. Spindrift wished she wouldn't do that, but of course Orchid couldn't make it stop. Instead, Spindrift filed inside the school as quickly as she could, with Max and Clémence behind her and the chattering of her other classmates adding to the noise.

She reached into her bag, finding the smooth glass with her fingertips. "I wish my teachers won't call on me today," she said.

"What was that?" Clémence asked.

"Nothing." Spindrift shook her head. Was it her imagination, or was the ball hotter now? The heat pulsed, a warning. Orchid couldn't grant that wish. Spindrift's head ached even harder as she tried to think of how to phrase her desire into a wish Orchid *could* grant.

She couldn't. Everything involved people not noticing her, or Spindrift herself being invisible. It wasn't fair that Orchid couldn't change what people thought or saw. It wasn't fair that she couldn't bring back Spindrift's parents so they could be a happy family again. What was the point in the crystal ball being only a little bit powerful? Think of the possibilities if Orchid could do anything!

Spindrift kicked the leg of her desk, and Clémence looked sharply at her from the next seat over. Pretending not to notice, Spindrift buried her head in her bag, as if she were looking for her book for the first lesson. "I wish for my books to hold all the answers today," she whispered. Just for today. Mostly she liked learning things for herself and wouldn't even let Grandfather help her with the answers when she was really stuck.

The book was the one she'd been reading on the history of Lux, and at the end of each chapter there were questions on what had been learned from it. Spindrift flipped to the correct page and let her gaze wander around the room, scowling at the back of Tristan's stupid head just for the fun of it.

She'd have a few wishes for him if Orchid could have granted them. She'd turn his eyebrows purple and glue his lips together and make his shoelaces come undone all day so that he tripped over them.

Hmmm. Perhaps that last one was possible, after all. Shoelaces were an object. Food was an object too. She could make everything he ate taste like the vegetables she knew he hated.

"Spin!" Clémence hissed, jerking Spindrift's attention to the teacher. Madame LaPierre was waiting expectantly, but Spindrift had no idea what she wanted. On Clémence's other side, Max was holding three fingers down low by his leg. Quickly, Spindrift looked at the third question on the page in front of her.

What are the names of the Seven Sages?

Spindrift cleared her throat and tried not to make it too obvious that she was reading directly from the paper, where the answers definitely weren't supposed to be. "Brand, Melia, Hector, Anise, Kumara, Perun, and Eleanor," she said, almost choking on the final name.

Eleanor. This book was where she'd read the name, the memory that had tickled at her when Orchid had told her what hers had once been.

"Good," said Madame LaPierre, nodding. "Pay more attention next time."

"I'm sorry," said Spindrift hoarsely. She couldn't escape now to ask Orchid about it, and no chance came after the lesson, either. Max and Clémence were on either side of her as they walked to the next. And so it went the rest of the day, until Spindrift began to suspect that her friends were keeping a close eye on her on purpose. Clémence kept giving her funny looks. The two of them knew Spindrift better than anyone except maybe Grandfather; they'd guessed something was different. If she wasn't very, very careful, people who didn't know her so well were going to suspect too.

"Let's go for a walk," said Clémence as soon as they were in the courtyard at the end of the afternoon. Spindrift frowned. She wanted to go home to the emptiness and solitude of her room, where she could ask Orchid all the questions she liked while Grandfather busied himself with customers downstairs.

She shook her head, and Clémence's brown eyes narrowed. "You've been acting odd all day, Spin. What's wrong?" Max looked at her too, waiting for an answer.

Spindrift opened her mouth. No, she didn't want to tell them yet. It was harder to keep Orchid a secret than she'd thought.

"Nothing," said Spindrift. "All right, I'll come."

Magothire Street was even busier than it had been that morning. Great glass windows displayed wares that would empty even the heaviest pocket of all its coins. Overhead, the gold and silver leaves of the trees glittered in the sunlight. It was warmer now, and while the dress wasn't itchy anymore, it was still made of thick wool. Spindrift insisted they stop for cups of lemonade from one of the vendors that littered the corners all the way down the great length of the street. Elegant ladies in gowns chattered under parasols about the newest opera opening, and men in suits leaned on their walking sticks. The city was alive with color, but all Spindrift could think of was a swirl of black ink, an orchid that bloomed when she looked at it.

CHAPTER SEVEN

Seven Sages

GRANDFATHER WAS COOKING. SPINDRIFT HEARD sizzling in a heavy pan, smelled butter and garlic and an herb she couldn't identify because she didn't have his nose, his skill for these things. Had her mother been a skilled cook? Had they eaten well on the *Masdevallia*, or had its crew lived on burned fish and raw vegetables purchased from the markets in the ports they'd visited?

No, definitely not. Emilie would have kept the entire ship well fed; Grandfather would have insisted she learn before ever letting her leave, just as he took every opportunity now to teach Spindrift how to bring ingredients together into a meal befitting the fanciest restaurant.

The crystal ball was still at the bottom of Spindrift's bag, waiting for the moment when Spindrift was sure she was alone. Now. Her fingers closed around it. "Orchid?" she said. "It's safe to come out."

The black ink was already swirling by the time Spindrift got her hand out of the bottom of the bag, and a moment later Orchid was hovering in the air above her, dress dancing in the draftless room.

"Yes, Spindrift?" she asked, smiling. "Do you have a wish?"

"I have a question."

The smile narrowed, just a little. "Go on."

It had been burning on Spindrift's lips all day. Finally she could ask it, and now her stomach tightened. What if the name was simply coincidence and Orchid laughed at her for thinking what she thought?

Oh well. Spindrift had never much cared if people laughed at her. Even Tristan only bothered her because he was so nasty about it. People laughed at things that were different, that they didn't understand, and she was more than happy to be special, unusual. "Are you one of the Seven Sages?"

Orchid's eyebrows rose, but she looked almost . . . impressed? "I was," she said. "Eleanor, the Seventh Sage. But I was human then, a person just like you. As we aged, we started to wonder how we might preserve ourselves so that we could continue to build the world around us—if not to do it ourselves, then at least to help those who came after. It was Melia who thought of the orchids, for they had been seen as magical in the land she came from, before the seven of us joined forces. Brand fashioned the crystals. Kumara came up with the rules, as we were aware, even then, of the lure of power and of what might happen if any one of us could grant too broad a wish."

"That's why you can only control objects!" said Spindrift, perhaps a little too loudly. Something crashed in the kitchen, and she put her finger to her lips to silence herself as much as Orchid while she listened for footsteps that didn't come.

"Yes," said Orchid when Spindrift gestured for her to go on. "Exactly. The others control . . . other things."

So, the others were orchids too, in crystal balls just like this one. And they were out there somewhere in the world. "What other things?"

"Brand is the red orchid, with the power of life and death, healing and injury. As a living sage he was a doctor. Melia is orange. A great warrior in her day, capable of commanding armies of thousands, though she was always one for peace. She can control the physical bodies of people—and animals, too, I suppose, though I'm not sure what use it is to move a cow from one field to another."

Spindrift laughed.

"Hector, our philosopher, controls emotions. He is yellow. Should someone wish it, he could turn your laugh just then into tears of the worst heartbreak. We were all given roles according to our gifts in life, you see. Anise, the green orchid, can alter time. She was a witch, particularly skilled at ensuring the cycles of the seasons ran smoothly. Kumara, blue, was an alchemist. Wishes asked of him concern all those things we cannot properly see nor explain. Magic, in other words. Perun, a warlock gifted at weather spells, is the purple of the clouds before a terrible storm. And me. I was an artificer. I could fix or create any object asked of me, and I still can."

"And together you built Lux."

"Together we built the world," Orchid corrected gently. "But Lux was our crowning achievement, our last great city. It was here that we grew old and here that we transformed ourselves."

"Where are the others?" Spindrift asked, and Orchid shrugged, making her airy, inky dress ripple.

"I do not know. They could be in Lux, or they could be flung to the farthest reaches of the world."

"Thank you," said Spindrift. The sounds from the kitchen were dying down, and she thought she heard the clink of silverware. "I'll have more wishes later."

Orchid nodded, withdrawing back into her crystal as quickly as she'd bloomed. Spindrift went over to the window to kneel on its seat and stare out across the city. Night was just falling; she could see where the lamplighters had been and the patches of darkness they had yet to reach. Out there people were going about their perfectly normal lives, cooking or reading or tending to their precious plants. Others might be dressing for dinner or the theater, or admiring the windows of Magothire Street. Boats bobbed on the river; alchemists worked late in their workshops.

It all looked different now. She sat at this window almost every day or evening, but now she saw the touches of the Sages everywhere, and not only in the arches scattered across the city or the thought of Sages' Hill rising behind her.

Footsteps creaked along the hallway floor, and she ran to open her door before Grandfather reached it. "Time to wash your hands," he said, looking past her into her room. His eyes narrowed as they lit on something, and a thrill of fear shot through Spindrift like lightning. He was so good with objects, he practically only had to see one to know what it could do, its history. Not unlike Orchid herself.

"Were you playing with that?" he asked, pointing at the crystal ball.

"Yes," she said, hoping her voice was steady, that he wouldn't guess.

He nodded. "Well, put it away for now. Wash and come to the table, and after we eat we have more letters to read."

The letters, she thought as water splashed into the sink. Her mother's letters, which spoke of her search for something. Perhaps she'd found it: a crystal ball so valuable, so precious, that the night of that terrible storm she'd put it into the boat with Spindrift rather than letting it fall to the bottom of the ocean.

The brass key shone in Grandfather's palm, and the lock on the box of letters snapped open. He rubbed his forehead as he straightened, his face shadowed with pain.

"Are you all right?" Spindrift asked him. She didn't like to see him in pain. It reminded her that he was old.

"Oh, yes, *chérie*. My head simply aches, that is all. Come, let us read a few of these before it is time to sleep. Now, where were we . . . ?" His fingers found the slip of red card, and he removed the letter immediately behind it. He gave the envelope to Spindrift and sat down on the couch beside her to read over her shoulder. Emilie's careful, precise handwriting was becoming familiar to Spindrift. She'd recognize it anywhere now. This letter was thinner than the one they'd read the previous evening, and Spindrift hoped that meant her parents hadn't encountered any more pirates. On the other hand, if she was right and the black orchid was in fact what her parents had been searching for, this note probably didn't say so. Such news would be pages and pages of detail. Still, Spindrift tried not to seem too impatient as she pulled the letter free.

2nd day of the Month of Feasts, in the Year of the Wind
S 51°41'40", W 51°51'10"

Dearest Papa,
After the excitement of my last letter, I am afraid there is not much to report. We spent quite some time having the ship repaired and have moved a few small items of cargo from one island to another, but I think the long, hot months have made us all listless and sleepy. Roland, our charming new quartermaster, threw himself into the ocean yesterday simply for something to do. It took three crewmen to fish him out again.

Speaking of fish, I am quite tired of eating it. Even in ports it is most often the fare available. I

long for your cooking, and for the lights of the city.
I will see if I can arrange to visit soon.
    Love,
    Emilie

Wordlessly, Grandfather handed Spindrift the next. His eyes were nearly closed, the lines in his face deep and etched with discomfort.

11th day of the Month of Eternity, in the Year of the Wind
N 69°40'58", E 18°56'34"

Dearest Papa,
It was such a wrench to leave you and Lux. I miss you already, but am happy to be back with Theo and on the ocean where I belong. The gunner has been teaching me to fire the cannon in case we are set upon by pirates again; I'm glad I know how to do it, even if I wish it weren't so very loud.

    We are far north now, and the bitter winds grow stronger every day. Excellent for the sails, but they make me wish it were still summer. I can barely feel my fingers on the wheel when it's my turn to take it.

*Our stores are full of tallow candles and other provi-
sions, though, so do try not to worry too much. When
we next dock I will send this letter and any special
objects I can find there, as I've heard rumors of some
talented artificers at our destination.*

Love,
Emilie

"Did she send things back to you?"

Grandfather winced, then nodded. "This and that.
Some very interesting small trinkets that were quickly
sold. *Chérie*, if you do not mind, I must go and lie down."

"What can I do? Shall I send for a physician? Would
you like a cup of tea?"

He shook his head, the movement clearly causing him
great pain. "No physician, my dear, but a cup of tea would
be most welcome."

Spindrift ran to the kitchen, realizing too late that her
pounding footsteps on the wooden floor were probably
most *un*welcome. Quietly as she could, she prepared a
cup and saucer while the water boiled. She snatched the
kettle from the flame the instant it began to whistle and
counted silently the precise number of minutes and seconds Grandfather decreed made the perfect cup of tea.

It was strange to be looking after him; more often it

was the other way around, when she fell ill with some malady or other she'd picked up at school. Spindrift tiptoed into his room and found him already in his small bed, the covers pulled up to his chin and his head back on the pillow. The tea would go cold, she was sure. Creeping out again, she found a soft cloth and soaked it in cold water. Grandfather groaned appreciatively when she laid it on his forehead, and Spindrift smiled, though he didn't see it. She closed the door softly behind her.

The apartment suddenly felt very large, and she very alone in it. The clock on the parlor wall said it was still a generous hour before her bedtime. She could read a book. She could read . . .

Her eyes went to the box on the couch. The fact that despite his headache, Grandfather had taken the time to lock it made Spindrift desperate to open it again, to find out why he was rationing her mother's letters so carefully. She didn't know where he kept the key.

But she didn't need to.

"Orchid!" she said, her hand closing around the crystal ball. She'd thought about hiding the box somewhere else, no longer beneath her bed, but Grandfather might find that more suspicious if he went looking.

The flower bloomed. "Hello, Spindrift," said Orchid. "What can I do for you?"

"I wish for you to follow me," said Spindrift. She kept the ball in her hand and walked swiftly but as quietly as possible back to the parlor. She pointed at the box of letters. "I wish for a key to that."

A key appeared in the lock.

"Thank you," said Spindrift. She held up the orb again, and with a sigh and a swirl of black ink, Orchid returned to it.

Spindrift turned the key. There was the red card marking the place she and Grandfather had reached. She leaned over the box, her fingertips running over the edges of the envelope. The most recent ones were at the back; she hoped the ones she was looking for weren't the last ones her mother sent.

With thumb and forefinger, she held a place several inches in and removed a letter. It was tricky to pull the paper free with one hand, but Grandfather would notice if any letters were out of order. She glanced at the date at the top in her mother's neat hand. *The Month of Mothers, in the Year of the Crows.* Three years before Spindrift was born. Too early. She put that one back.

The Month of Endless Fire, the Year of Echoes, read the next. Two years before Spindrift was born.

The next two she chose were both from the Year of the Familiar, the second one sharing the happy news.

Spindrift stuffed its envelope at an angle in the box to mark her place and held the precious letter in both hands.

> *Dearest Papa,*
> *I can barely contain myself. I don't know how I'll wait until we reach our next port before sending this, though of course I must. Theo and I are going to have a baby—you are going to be a grand-père! I know already what you'll say, that I must return to Lux and that the ocean is no place for an infant. Let us not worry about that yet, all right? I have seen a physician, and the baby should come in the Month of Rains, so we have plenty of time. If it is a boy he will be named after Theo, and if it is a girl I will name her after Maman.*
>
> *I hope you are as thrilled by this as we are. Please forgive me if I don't do quite so much hunting for artifacts in the coming months. I find myself easily tired now. Our little mystery will thus be put on hold for a time. I'm sure you understand.*
> *Love,*
> *Emilie*

Spindrift stared at the words for a long time, until tears welled in her eyes. She moved the letter aside so

they wouldn't fall and smudge the ink. Even such a small thing, Grandfather might notice. He had told her many times of her parents' joy when they'd discovered she was to be born, but it was different reading it in her mother's own voice. She knew they hadn't returned to Lux, that she'd been born on the ocean and stayed there. The first time Grandfather set eyes on her had been after she was rescued.

It simply wasn't fair that they'd been taken from her when they'd been so happy to have her. And it simply wasn't fair that Orchid couldn't bring them back when it was the one thing she wanted most. The three of them would set out on the ocean again, on a ship even grander than the *Masdevallia*, searching out objects for Grandfather's shop. The fantasy filled her with warmth that spread all the way to her fingers and toes.

She reached for another letter.

CHAPTER EIGHT

Archenemy

28th day of the Month of Rains, in the Year of the Stars
N 43°19'17", W 1°59'8"

Dearest Papa,
It's a girl! As promised, I named her after Maman,
but I'm afraid she doesn't hear it very much. Theo
calls her Spindrift, and it's easy to see why. She's a
wisp of a thing, as light as the mist over the waves,
and her hair is as dark as a storm. She's so beautiful.
I think I've never loved anything so much. Even
you! I'm sorry. She was born seven days ago. This
is the first time I've had a chance to sit down with
quill and paper.

The entire crew dotes on her except for Philippe— our first mate is a grumpy sort, but I think he's fond of her in his own gruff way and just doesn't know how to show it. You will adore her, and I promise I will bring her to visit as soon as I'm able. We stayed in port for the birth as a precaution before beginning our journey. If all is well, we will set sail in a day or two, though we will be making some stops on the way. Our little mystery is calling to me, or more accurately, I have heard whispers that speak of it.

You're going to tell me I should rest. At least, you would if you were here. I promise I feel well up to the adventure, and worried the opportunity will slip through our grasp if I leave it for too long. Who knows, it may already be too late! For both of us, and Theo and beautiful little Spindrift, I must try.

Love,

Emilie

This time, Spindrift gazed at the letter longer than necessary for a different reason. She'd searched through the letters looking for this particular one, knowing it must exist, and yes, this one kept the warm glow burning inside her—it was about her—but there was something else, too. A few something elses. She'd never known that it was her father who first called her Spindrift. It seemed an odd thing for Grandfather to keep from her. But it made sense; *Spindrift* was a word in her father's native tongue, not Grandfather's. More important, however, her mother had mentioned the mystery, clearly still unsolved. She hadn't found the black orchid yet, and she would not be Grandfather's kin if she turned her back on a mystery. When an object was brought to him, if its abilities were unknown, he'd scarcely sleep until he discovered them. On the rare occasions they appeared to be useless, he never stopped wondering whether there was some test he could have performed that would have revealed its secrets.

The very next letter was dated only a few weeks later.

5th day of the Month of Fools, in the Year of the Stars
N 38°42'50", W 9°8'22"

Dearest Papa,
As I suspected, I was too late. We made our first stop, and while there seemed to be lingering echoes of one of the things we seek, it was gone by the time we arrived. We have been pointed toward a new destination, with little choice but to go investigate there. Spindrift—the name seems to have stuck—is a jewel, the most precious thing the Masdevallia

has ever carried. Even Philippe is coming around to her. The motion of the boat soothes her few cries and sends her straight to sleep. Theo is a doting father. He tells her stories of life on the seas no matter how often I remind him that she's too young to understand.

Back to our mystery, I feel now as if I am chasing soap bubbles that pop the moment I get too near. Our mission is made all the more difficult by its secrecy; only a few of us aboard know what the Masdevallia's *true purpose has become. It's safer that way. To the knowledge of the rest of the crew, we are doing what we have always done, moving cargo from place to place. It is a useful deception, but it would be a relief to be able to speak more freely.*

I can only hope, as I'm sure you do, that in the end we will be rewarded for our efforts. I will be heartbroken if the rest of them turn out not to exist, but I'm sure they must. There are too many signs in too many places. The marks on the arches are proof enough.

Spindrift needs me now. I must go.

Love,

Emilie

The marks on the arches—did she mean the Sages' arches here in Lux? Spindrift couldn't remember ever having seen marks on them, but she couldn't claim she'd ever looked. Even more interesting was that her mother obviously hadn't found the black orchid at the time she'd sent this letter and that Grandfather clearly knew precisely what Emilie was seeking. There were at least fifty more letters dated after this one; Emilie must have written more frequently in the final year of her life, once every week or two it looked like. There were just as many dated before it, too, between it and the red card that marked where Spindrift and Grandfather had reached together. She couldn't read all of them tonight. For the first time since she sat down, Spindrift noticed the soft ticking of the clock on the wall. It was past her bedtime now. If Grandfather woke and came to check on her, he'd want to know why she wasn't yet asleep. He'd also wonder how she'd opened the box when he still had the key.

Her mouth was dry, and she regretted not making herself a cup of tea when she'd made one for Grandfather, but she remembered what he'd said about not wanting the letters ruined. It would be just her luck to spill the cup when she was busy reading the letters without his permission.

Now that she knew she could read them whenever she liked, thanks to the key she'd wished for, she didn't need to get through them all at once. She *wanted* to, but her eyes were beginning to feel heavy and she was a bit afraid that if she kept reading she'd miss something important.

Maybe . . . just one more.

She placed the letter she'd just read back in the box and took out the next. It felt thin, a scrap of paper put in an envelope and folded over and over until it fit in the belly of a tiny brass bird.

1st day of the Month of Endless Fire, in the Year of the Stars
S 18°09', E 49°25'

Dearest Papa,
We found one. The red one. It works, though not as well as the black does for me, which is no great surprise. I do not have the same connection to the red, and still it does my bidding within its limitations. Those limitations both fascinate and frustrate me; I must see how far I may push them. I tried with this one simply to wish for all the others, and of course it didn't work. I must seek them out myself.
Love,
Emilie

Spindrift licked her lips and read the letter over in a whisper that wouldn't disturb Grandfather and his head-ache. The red one. At the time of writing this, Emilie already had the black orchid Spindrift had been so sure was the thing her mother searched for. She didn't know what her mother had meant by a connection, but Spindrift was as certain as she could be that her mother had pos-sessed the black orchid for some time before this letter was dated. In the previous ones she'd spoken of a mystery unsolved, surely the time to mention the black orchid if it were a new thing. No, Emilie already had it when she set sail on the *Masdevallia*; if she'd found it in her early days on the ship, Spindrift would have read about it with Grandfather.

If the rest of them turn out not to exist.

She hadn't been hunting for the black orchid she'd tucked into the little boat with Spindrift. She'd been hunting for them all. Red, orange, yellow, green, blue, purple. And she'd found at least one, which for some reason hadn't made the trip to land with Spindrift in the furor of the terrible storm.

Grandfather thought she was spending the afternoon with Clémence and Max. Clémence and Max thought she had gone home to Grandfather. A slight pang of guilt at having deceived them all lingered in Spindrift's chest after she left school the following afternoon, but by the time she'd turned the corner and begun her long walk toward the one of the arches, it was gone. Orchid was in the bag over her shoulder, ready to grant Spindrift's wishes if any occurred to her.

She'd looked at a map and knew the arches formed a rough circle around the city, with the final one on the hilltop near the center. She was saving the one on the hill above the shop for last because it was closest to home; she'd inspect them all and be back in time for whatever delicious dinner Grandfather had planned for the evening. He wouldn't suspect a thing.

On the street around her, shops were beginning to shutter for the evening. People in aprons were sweeping the streets, folding away awnings, removing delicacies from plate-glass windows. Nobody paid any heed to Spindrift, a girl with a schoolbag who was walking home for all they knew.

The arch was at a crossroads ahead, farther away than it had first seemed to Spindrift. No matter how quickly she walked, she didn't feel like she was getting any closer. There weren't so many shops or people around now, and those there were had a distinct air of shabbiness. She'd definitely left Magothire Street behind, with its palace and music halls and hothouses, the gilt and the scent of gold. This was a part of the city she'd never seen, stone walls smeared with soot and grime, the streetlights still old-fashioned gas instead of the fancy new filament lamps. The carriages trundling down the road creaked and shook, pulled by tired horses. Cracked paving stones wobbled beneath her feet.

Finally, the arch was closer. She waited at the corner until it was safe to cross to the island in the center of the crossroads. The arch was dirty, too; its thick piers, twice as wide as Spindrift was tall, were nearly black.

Her mother had said there were signs on the arches. Spindrift craned her neck to look up at the keystone, but there was nothing there. She walked through the arch and stood beneath it, the sounds from the street muffled slightly here. Again she turned her head every which way, searching.

"What are you doing, little girl?" asked a voice. Spindrift whirled to face an old woman clothed in rags, beaming at Spindrift with a toothless smile. Spindrift stepped backward.

"N-nothing," she stammered.

"Doesn't look like nothing to me." The woman's eyes narrowed. "Looks to me like you're lost, standing here in my house in your fancy dress and pretty shoes."

Her house? She lived here? Spindrift glanced down at herself. It was only her ordinary school dress and simple flat shoes. They did have silver buckles, though.

"Here," said Spindrift, leaning down and wrenching one of the buckles free. She held it out, her hand trembling a bit. "Is there a mark somewhere on this arch? If you help me find it, I'll give you this."

"A mark, you say. Why, as a matter of fact, you may be in luck. Let me see that."

Spindrift moved her hand forward a few inches, and the buckle was snatched away. "This will do. Come," the woman ordered. She led Spindrift out of the other side of the arch and rubbed at the grime on a spot just above Spindrift's head.

"Thank you," said Spindrift, her mouth dry.

"They tried to take the pretty stones, but I wouldn't let them. It's my home, I said, my pretty stones."

"Yes," said Spindrift, not listening.

The mark was a circle, about the same diameter as her crystal ball. Something deep inside Spindrift's brain didn't think that was a coincidence, but only because of what was inside. She didn't know what it was made of, but there was no mistaking what it was meant to be.

Inlaid into the grubby gray stone was a red orchid.

"Thank you," Spindrift said again. "I have to go now."

She turned and ran across the street, tripping over her unbuckled shoe and narrowly escaping an oncoming cart. She paid no attention to where she was running, simply ran until she thought she was alone. She was in a short alley somewhere behind the main road, and she couldn't see or hear anyone.

She leaned against the wall, breathing heavily. She'd known it must be there and yet it was still a shock to see it, her suspicions fully confirmed. The red orchid of Brand, First of the Seven Sages. Her mother had found the actual one in its crystal ball and somehow lost it again, or put it somewhere for safekeeping. Perhaps it had fallen to the bottom of the ocean with the *Masdevallia*, and that thought sent a strange, roiling sickness through Spindrift's belly. The orchids should never suffer such a fate.

Spindrift frowned at herself. Her parents shouldn't have suffered so, either. But it was different. *Her* orchid had said she couldn't die, and what a horrible fate, to be trapped inside a crystal ball and resting on the ocean floor where no one would ever find it and set the orchid free for even long enough to make a wish.

"Orchid," she said, casting another look up and down the alley to ensure she was alone. "It's safe. You can come out."

The orchid was almost the same shade as the lengthening shadows of the alley when she appeared, darkness upon darkness, her pale face stark against the grubby brick wall behind her. "Hello, Spindrift," she said. "Such a pretty name. Do you have a wish?"

Really, Spindrift had just been struck by the urge to let Orchid stretch. Though Spindrift had wished for several small, silly things that day whenever she'd found moments alone before breakfast or between lessons, she'd kept her inside the ball to do so. She should probably think of a wish.

There were six more arches to visit, and now Spindrift had a broken shoe. She could wish for it to be mended, but still she suddenly didn't fancy walking all that way. "You can't move me from one place to another, can you?" she asked.

"Alas." Orchid shook her head. "No, I cannot. Melia could, if she were here."

"The orange one?"

Orchid nodded.

Spindrift recalled the last note she'd read from her mother. "And I can't use you to wish for another one, even though they're objects?"

Again Orchid shook her head, and was it Spindrift's imagination, or did her crimson lips thin a little? "No," said Orchid. "When we made ourselves, we made sure that was impossible."

"Why?"

Orchid's drifty, wispy arms folded across herself. "For the same reason we limited our individual capabilities. It is not a good idea to give a person too much power too easily. Think of it, Spindrift. You have me, and with me you may change, summon, banish any object you can think of at will. Now, think of what I told you of all the others and how you might combine our gifts. There is nothing you wouldn't be able to do."

Oh. Spindrift needed to think about that for a while, and she didn't want to do it standing here in this alley. A stench from a pile of rotting vegetables was beginning to drift over and wrinkle her nose, and she had other places to be now. "I wish for a pair of the wings Grandfather keeps in his shop." Hopefully he wasn't standing beside their spot right this minute to see them vanish.

This Orchid could do, and easily. Spindrift had barely blinked and they were in her hands, the red pair Clémence had worn recently. "I wish for you to send my schoolbag to my room." Then she thought of something else. "And I wish for a warm cloak, a long heavy one with a big hood. Not itchy."

A thick, soft cloak settled around her shoulders. Spindrift put the wings on over it and pulled the hood up over her head so that it almost covered her face. "Thank you," she said, holding up the crystal ball so Orchid could disappear back inside it. The cloak had a very convenient pocket sewn into the inside, fastened with a button so nothing could fall out. Sure that the orchid was safe, Spindrift pulled a small lever on the leather strap near her shoulder and felt herself rising from the dank ground, between the walls of the buildings and up, up, over the rooftops of Lux. Her map was in her bag, sent back home, but from up here she could see the arches, and the nearest was at the corner of Hollow Street and the palace gardens.

She'd flown like this many times before; it never stopped being fun, or windy. Her eyes watered and the city below her blurred to pinpoints of light where windows glowed and the lamplighters had been to do their work. The cloak rippled and billowed like Orchid's black dress, but the wings' straps held it close enough to her body to keep her warm.

The palace gardens were an enormous expanse of lush green just off Magothire Street, with the palace itself rising in their center, surrounded by rosebushes and lilies and tall, silver-leafed trees. The palace was a pure white that caught the sun in daytime and glowed like bleached bone in moonlight. Now, at the far end of afternoon, it was tinged a faint pink by sunset, like a giant rosewater meringue.

Spindrift flew over it and to the far side of the gardens, lowering herself slowly as the Arch of the Second Sage came into view. As she descended, she thought it might have made more sense for the palace to be beside the Arch of the First Sage, where she'd just been, or the Seventh Sage, which stood atop Sages' Hill. Then again, perhaps not. The Second Sage was Melia, commander of armies in war and peace. Wasn't that the same as a queen?

Spindrift's feet touched down gently on the clipped grass just in front of the arch, and she walked the rest of the way, ignoring both the curious stares of some evening visitors to the garden and the impulse to tell them that if they wanted such a pair of wings for their very own, they only had to visit Grandfather's shop on Nightbrick Lane. Knowing what she was looking for made it easier to find. Another circle around another orchid, this one picked out in orange stone.

She didn't linger. Next she flew to Mulberry Orchard, halfway across Lux. Though it was no longer an orchard proper, there were still mulberry trees on the short road it had become, just beginning to bear their fruit. Spindrift and Grandfather came here every summer to pick them, and ate themselves sick on mulberry pies for days after, warm and sweet and covered in cream. She'd gone out of order, flying to the next nearest one, and this was the Arch of the Fourth Sage, Anise, who could grant wishes that would alter time. Spindrift's orchid had said Anise was a witch adept at bringing each season at the right moment.

The next was purple, then yellow, then blue, the orchids painting their rainbow across the city. Finally, there was only one left.

Spindrift landed on top of Sages' Hill.

She almost didn't come, so sure was she of what she'd find, but she had to see it. It was unthinkable to go home without completing the set and let the unfinished feeling nag at her the way the itchy neck of her dress used to. The full weight of darkness had fallen while Spindrift visited the arches, and now night was as black as her cloak as she stood atop the hill above Grandfather's shop. The river rippled, a black ribbon. Lamps shone, picking out the lines of the streets below.

But there were no lamps up here. Spindrift squinted in the gloom, the arch forming itself from shadows as her eyes adjusted. The stone was rough against her fingers, as she searched her way around the arch.

There, just above her head, was a circle with a black orchid inside it, faint moonlight glinting off the obsidian leaves.

Spindrift exhaled. It was nice to be right.

Then she froze. From behind her had come the unmistakable sound of a footstep. It was one thing to visit the arches in daylight, with people all around, but anyone finding her now would surely wonder what a young girl was doing up here in the dark, her arms stretched so she could press her fingers to the sign of the orchid on the arch.

Another footstep came. Slowly, Spindrift turned, preparing to run.

It was *him*. His face was a few short feet away, just around the corner of the arch, and she remembered it so clearly in the musty peace of Grandfather's shop, the strange smile, the smoothness of his voice as he made his request.

He wanted the black orchid.

Desperate, Spindrift reached for the crystal ball and buried her head inside the cloak. "Orchid," she whispered, quiet as she could. "Can you make this cloak invisible?"

Spindrift didn't know whether it had worked until he stepped closer. He was wearing the same dark suit, the same odd expression. His eyes were fixed on the orchid just above Spindrift's head; he could not see her.

He was close enough that Spindrift could smell his breath. She stifled a shriek, and her poised muscles sprang free, releasing her to run just as she'd planned.

She felt her mistake with her next step, her stockinged foot landing on the cobbles that surrounded the arch, her broken shoe left behind. The shoe, no longer beneath her cloak, was no longer protected by her wish.

"Who's there?" demanded the man, his voice breaking the spell of silence on Sages' Hill.

Spindrift held her breath. As silently as she could, she turned to see the man bend down and pick up her shoe. He turned it over in his hands, his head tilted to one side.

"I know you're here," he said gently. "Show yourself, little girl. You see, I have seen these shoes before, and I know of only one little girl who might be interested in the story of the orchids."

Spindrift bit her tongue.

"And that means you lied to me," he said in a dangerous whisper. "I came and I asked you, and you told me you had never seen the thing I described."

Unseen, Spindrift shook her head. No! She hadn't lied to him. The crystal ball hadn't shown its secrets until after he'd come to the shop. Somehow, she didn't think that this explanation would matter to him, even if she revealed herself to give it.

"I know where to find you," he said. "And then I know where to find the last one. If you show yourself to me now, I will not be forced to do anything I might regret to you or your grandfather. Show yourself, Spindrift. Give me your orchid, and there will be peace."

CHAPTER NINE
A Secret Shared

S HE BARELY REMEMBERED TO WISH herself visible on the shop's doorstep before bursting through the door. Grandfather looked up from the counter with a warm smile, and Spindrift couldn't understand why he was smiling. Didn't he know they were in danger?

No, he didn't. Of course he didn't. She had run from the hilltop a second after the man had said her name—how had he known her name?—but now that she was home, she didn't know what to say, how to warn Grandfather of the peril they were in. She was certain the man must have heard her racing footsteps, but had he followed her? Was he, at this very moment, on the other side of the door?

"There you are," Grandfather said, coming out from

behind the counter. "I was beginning to wonder. Did you have fun with Clémence and Max? I really must call upon their parents about our little voyage."

It felt so long ago that she had told him the lie, and now she felt even worse about telling it. She was keeping so much from him, and right this minute she couldn't remember why. He was the cleverest person she knew. He would know how to fix everything. In order to fix it, however, she would have to tell him about the mess she'd made, the lies she'd told just because she'd wanted to keep the orchid all to herself.

He would be so disappointed in her. She'd always tried so hard to be a good granddaughter, to do what she was told and help him whenever she could, because it had been so nice of him to take her in when she had nobody else. She couldn't bear to tell him.

Maybe she didn't have to, not tonight. Perhaps there was a way to keep them safe for a little while longer. Perhaps she could find enough time to think.

"They're all right," she said finally. "Can we go upstairs? I'm starving."

"Of course, *chérie*. It's about time for me to be locking up anyway."

She didn't run ahead up the stairs. She waited to watch him seal the door against any dangers that might wander up Nightbrick Lane. They wouldn't find the shop by accident, and this time they would be the wrong kind of strange.

Her fingers closed around the crystal ball, still in the pocket of her cloak.

Spindrift had to word this carefully. According to the rules of the wishes, she couldn't actually stop the man from coming here. She couldn't wish for herself and Grandfather to be safe.

"Orchid," she whispered. "Stay inside."

"Yes, Spindrift?"

Grandfather was ahead of her, the creaking stairs masking the sound of Spindrift's voice—she hoped. "I wish . . ." She stopped.

"What do you wish?"

Grandfather had reached the top of the stairs and opened the door to their little apartment. Any instant now he'd notice Spindrift wasn't right behind him,

"I wish for this building to be as impenetrable as a fortress tonight," said Spindrift, soft as she could. Was a building an object? A thing? Or was it like the orchid herself, an object in which something lived?

"Well done," said Orchid.

She was so restless all evening even Grandfather noticed, asking her why she kept rising to look out the windows. Her dinner of roasted chicken and peppers fried in oil was as delicious as everything else Grandfather cooked, but mostly she pushed it around her plate with her fork. After they'd eaten, Grandfather got out the box of letters, and she tried hard to concentrate, really she did. It didn't help that she had to stop herself from asking him to skip ahead to where her mother began talking about the mystery.

She didn't sleep a wink, her thoughts racing through the night as she lay in the dark, her ears pricked for any strange noise. Sometime after midnight she thought she heard footsteps on the cobbles outside, but when she got up to look, Nightbrick Lane seemed as quiet as a grave.

She slept fitfully, half of her mind on unwelcome visitors, the other half on what she should do next. The light of dawn made the shadows much less frightening, and by the time she'd finished breakfast she was resolute.

Help, that was what she needed. Not from Grandfather— yet—but that meant leaving him alone. She kissed his cheek good-bye as if it were any ordinary day and stood outside the shop's front door, making a cascade of wishes so quickly Orchid nearly had a hard time keeping up. He might wonder why he got no customers, but that wasn't so unusual, out of the way as the shop was. Invisible under the cloak down to her second-best pair of shoes, Spindrift ran to school. It was important he not be any more suspicious than she already thought he was—for just a little while longer.

The moment Madame Dulac rang the heavy bell for the final time that afternoon, Spindrift dragged Clémence and Max into a corner of the courtyard, up against one of the high gray stone walls.

"I need to tell you both something," she whispered. "Can you come back home with me?"

"Yes!" said Clémence, and Max nodded eagerly. They both enjoyed exploring in Grandfather's shop, though Spindrift wasn't going to let them linger in there for long today. It might be better to go somewhere else to be alone, but she didn't want to stay away from Grandfather. She hoped her wishes had worked today.

They had to run to keep up with her. "Spin!" said Clémence, panting as they raced down Argent Avenue. "What is it? What's wrong?"

"Just wait," said Spindrift. She veered into Nightbrick Lane and up the hill, then stopped so abruptly Max crashed into her back and they both went toppling to the cobblestones. Books and quills and a crystal ball spilled out of her schoolbag, the latter bouncing over the stones and beginning to roll back down the hill.

"Catch that!" Spindrift yelled to Clémence, who chased after it, returning a few moments later with the orb in her hand. Spindrift snatched it from her and shoved it back into the bottom of her bag—a bit too quickly, judging from Clémence's affronted expression.

"Sorry," said Spindrift, bending down to pick up the other, unimportant things. "Max, are you all right?"

"Ouch," said Max, rubbing his knee. But he nodded, and together Spindrift and Clémence pulled him to his feet. *Now* Spindrift could look at the thing that had made her stop in the first place. They were outside one of the small hothouses, its glass windows giving a view of the controlled green wilderness within. On a shelf just on the other side of the glass, a single black orchid shivered atop a spindly stem.

Without a word to Clémence and Max, Spindrift pushed open the door. A bell tinkled, and from behind a jungle of tall plants, the red-haired woman Spindrift occasionally saw in the lane looked up.

"Oh, hello," she said. "I know you. How is your grandfather, my dear?"

"He's fine," said Spindrift. She hoped. "I wanted to ask"—she pointed at the flower—"about this."

"Striking, isn't it?" said the woman, coming over to join Spindrift, Clémence, and Max at the shelf. "An incredibly rare specimen. I should have it locked up, but I couldn't resist the urge to show it off for an hour or two.

You aren't the first to come in and ask about it, just in that time. Our hunters were very lucky to find one."

"Your orchid hunters," said Spindrift.

"A dangerous business, but one that yields such treasures," said the woman. "Fortune awaits those who find the most perfect or unusual plants. Fortune . . . or death."

"People *die* doing this?" Clémence asked.

"Oh, yes. Competition is fierce, and the environments in which the orchids grow are themselves often dangerous. It is not a quest for the fainthearted. It is a quest for the passionate. Those for whom the perfect *Cymbidium* or *Masdevallia* is worth whatever risk it takes to obtain it."

Masdevallia.

"How much for this one?" Spindrift asked quickly, silencing Max. She couldn't yet begin to wonder what that meant.

The woman frowned. "It is very expensive, I'm afraid. More than a little girl has, I'm sure."

Spindrift had a jar of coins in her bedroom, waiting for something she felt was worth spending them on. She slipped her hand into her bag, touching the glass within and whispering, and removed a heavy handful of gold.

Clémence and Max gaped at her.

• • •

Grandfather was safe—and happy, his expression quickly turning to pleasure at the sight of Clémence and Max behind Spindrift in the doorway. "I'll tell your parents you're here," he said, reaching for a clockwork bird. "Will you stay for supper?"

"Yes please!" said Max, and Clémence laughed.

The bird, its note within, was sent on its way. Only then did Grandfather seem to notice the plant in Spindrift's hands. He came around from behind the wooden counter and reached for it, withered fingers stroking the delicate black petals. For a moment he closed his eyes and took a deep breath. "Yes," he said, almost as if to himself. "All right. Go upstairs, you three. I will join you in a while. Not a single customer today, but I'll give it another hour or two."

There would be no customers, but he didn't need to know that. Spindrift led Clémence and Max up to the apartment and into the parlor, where she set the precious black orchid—the plant—gently down on a table. She sat on the floor and removed the *other* precious black orchid from her bag.

"Spin, what *is* going on?" Clémence asked, finding herself a seat and gesturing for Max to do the same. Their eyes were fixed on her, and she knew she had to answer— she wanted to answer—but it was so difficult to know where to start. Every time Spindrift herself thought she knew where the story started, another piece of the puzzle appeared.

Masdevallia.

Long ago, when they were old enough to ask why Spindrift lived with her grandfather, she'd told them about the storm, the shipwreck, her rescue. She'd shown them the crystal ball that seemed to be only a plaything, a trinket. It had been in the boat with her when she was rescued, she'd told them, and nothing had ever appeared in the middle of it.

She began with the day the man had visited the shop, which seemed much longer ago than it actually had been. So much had happened these past few days. She told Clémence and Max about beginning to read her mother's letters, which they already knew about, and about the night the orchid had bloomed, which they didn't. At this, both of their mouths dropped open, but they stayed silent, waiting for Spindrift to finish. The silence was more surprising from Clémence than it was from Max.

Some of her wishes sounded silly now that she was telling other people about them, in a slightly defensive tone. There hadn't been anything she'd wanted, except the one thing the orchid couldn't give her. That wasn't so true anymore now; she'd get to that. The wish for the key hadn't been silly, though not when she explained what she'd found in the letters and what she'd found on the arches the letters had led her to.

Her voice shook as she described the encounter with the strange man at the final arch, repeating the words that had played over and over again in her head all through a sleepless night. *I will not be forced to do anything I might regret to you or your grandfather.* She was so tired.

"Wish for something," said Max. "Something we can see."

It was only fair for him to ask. She dragged herself to her feet and held out her hand. Clémence returned the crystal ball. "Orchid," said Spindrift. "Come out, please."

Spindrift was used to it by now—the swirl of ink, the flower blooming, but Clémence and Max weren't. Astonished, they stared at the woman appearing before them, a smile on her face, her dress of ink and midnight dancing in the air.

"I wish . . ." Spindrift looked around. Her eyes lit on the pale-green silk wallpaper. "I wish the walls were blue." The color of oceans.

"Okay," said Max weakly after a second. "I believe you."

"You can wish for *anything*?" Clémence demanded.

"Not anything, but any *thing*, almost. My orchid can

control objects. When she was the Seventh Sage, she was an artificer. Thank you, Orchid."

"The orchids are the Sages?" Clémence and Max chimed together.

"They were."

"Wow," said Clémence. "Will it work for me?"

Spindrift almost didn't want to give her friend the crystal ball, though she, too, was curious about the answer. Reluctantly, she handed it over, with Orchid bloomed in the stale parlor air between them.

"I wish for . . . um . . ."

Sometimes it was harder than it looked. Spindrift grinned at Max.

"I wish for a black dress like yours," said Clémence to the orchid. And a black dress appeared around Clémence, swirling and shifting, but it wasn't the same. It flickered, faded in and out before disappearing completely. Clémence's face fell.

"Why didn't it work properly?"

"I don't know," said Spindrift honestly. "She said sometimes she is given, and sometimes she is taken. I think it has to be yours for it to work right. Thank you, Orchid." The flower bloomed in reverse, back into the crystal ball.

Them believing her was the first step. Just the first. Grandfather was still in danger, and there was still a mystery to solve. And she had to solve it. She knew that now. The crystal ball was the only thing she had from her parents; she wasn't going to give it to some strange man. The only other way to protect Grandfather was to find out why the strange man wanted it.

A suspicion curled at the pit of her stomach. She thought she already knew. The arches had told her, and the man himself had confirmed it. So had her mother's letters.

"The man is trying to collect them all," she said. "Orchid told me that together they are even more powerful than one of them is alone. I'm not sure she meant to tell me that, but she did. He said . . ." She closed her eyes, remembering his presence at the arch, his breath so close to her. "He said he knew I had this one and that he knew where the last one was." Which really meant he already had the last one, even if it wasn't actually in his possession.

Perhaps he was busy fetching it now and would come back for Spindrift's when he was finished.

"What do you think happens when they're all together?" asked Clémence. "Or d'you think he just wants the complete set, because collectors can be like that?"

"Well, if each one of them controls something important," said Max, "together they can control everything. The Sages were people, the most powerful people in the world."

"She's not a person now," said Clémence. "She's a piece of magic."

No, she wasn't a person, but Spindrift was struck by the idea that Orchid did have feelings, of a kind. It must be a very lonely existence, trapped inside a crystal ball all the time, summoned only when someone wanted something from her. Spindrift had hardly any family, but at least she had Grandfather, and Clémence and Max, too, who felt like family.

Somewhere in her mother's letters must be more answers. With Max's and Clémence's help she could get through them three times as quickly as she could alone. Her mother had been looking for the orchids, that much was clear.

The box was in Grandfather's bedroom, the key Spindrift wished for in the pocket of her black wool dress. She carried the box back into the parlor and set it down in front of Clémence and Max. Once again the key fit perfectly into the lock.

The floor shook, and from below came a terrible crash.

CHAPTER TEN

Son of the Red Orchid

GRANDFATHER!" SPINDRIFT FELL THROUGH THE door to the shop, having nearly flown down the stairs. Clémence and Max were behind her, and the three of them stared at the scene before them, Grandfather still behind the counter and a man—*him*—standing next to a million shards of glass and bits of twisted silver from a fallen cabinet.

"How did you get in here?" Spindrift demanded. She thought she'd made Grandfather safe. Her chest hurt from fear.

"I am all right, *chérie*," said Grandfather calmly.

"I have wishes too, little girl," said the man. "More of them than you do."

Spindrift felt Grandfather's eyes upon her. The skin of her face warmed uncomfortably, but now was not the time to explain. "Give it to me and I will leave."

"No, Roland," said Grandfather, stepping out from behind the counter with surprising speed, putting himself between Spindrift and the man. "We will give you nothing."

"Move aside! I am the Son of the Red Orchid. They belong to me!"

"No," said Grandfather again. "I know what you seek, and it will never be yours. I promise you that."

The man raised one hand, a gloved finger pointing. The other drew a crystal ball from his pocket. "I wish—"

Grandfather waved *his* hand. A swarm of clockwork birds, the same as the one he'd sent with the message to Clémence and Max's parents, flew from the shelf and swarmed the man, metal beaks pecking at every part of him they could reach.

Another cabinet exploded, a rain of glass falling. Blood beaded on Grandfather's cheek.

"Go, Spindrift!" he ordered, but she couldn't move. A sword flew from a rack on the back wall, its hilt landing in Grandfather's waiting palm. It was an old sword, imbued with protective magic, and he'd forbidden her from ever touching it, it was so sharp.

"I wish to have that sword," said the man. Quickly as it had come, it left Grandfather's grip. Spindrift screamed.

"Don't worry, Spindrift! I said go!"

She still couldn't move, only watch as one by one, Grandfather summoned objects from shelves and cases. He knew the objects in the shop better than anyone, their abilities and shortfalls. He knew which ones could protect him from the sword slicing through the air.

"I killed your daughter," said the man, grinning. "Do you not think I will do the same to you? Give me the orchid!"

"Never!"

The man looked at his crystal ball. "I wish—"

For an old man in slippers, Grandfather moved like lightning, taking advantage of the temporary distraction to wrest back the sword. He pressed its razor tip to the man's chest. For the first time, Spindrift saw a flicker of fear in the man's cold eyes.

"Leave," said Grandfather slowly, dangerously. "Leave before I run you through for the things you've done and to stop you doing more. Were we alone, I would have no hesitation. If you come back, I assure you my reservations will leave me."

The man stood fast, then yelped in pain. Blood bloomed like a flower on the white silk of his shirt.

"Leave," said Grandfather again.

Spindrift stood in shock as the door opened, closed again. As if it were any ordinary afternoon, Grandfather went over and turned the heavy key in the lock, his slippers crunching over the broken glass.

Only then did he turn to Spindrift, his eyes flitting from her to Clémence and Max and back to his granddaughter again.

"Well," he said. "It seems we should have a little talk, *chérie*. Let us all go put the kettle on."

Nodding dumbly, Spindrift spun and followed her friends up the stairs, checking every few steps that Grandfather was still behind her. He didn't look angry. She didn't know what to call the expression on his face. The blood had dripped down his cheek, a bright red ribbon ending at his collar. She stood in the kitchen doorway as he arranged four cups and saucers on a tray, with spoons and sugar and milk.

The kettle whistled. Clémence and Max were looking at each other, communicating with their eyes as they sometimes did. Max shook his head.

"Come, now," said Grandfather, leading the way to the parlor. He took in the scene there: the box of letters that had been in his bedroom, and a crystal ball on the floor. He looked, too, at the black orchid on the table, alive and perfect, its pointy leaves a lush green, its roots curled over the edge of the pot.

"It came to you," he said, putting the tray down on the table. It wasn't a question. "When?"

"A few—" Spindrift swallowed. "A few days ago."

"I don't suppose there is any reason to send you two away," he said to Clémence and Max, "as I assume she has told you everything she knows?"

They nodded in unison.

"But she does not know everything. Neither do I, for that matter, but I can possibly provide some new information. Everybody, sit."

Spindrift felt as if she'd never truly seen Grandfather before. Her entire life he had been an old man, shuffling in his slippers between his beloved objects and cups of tea. Now he was hoisting swords and he knew about the orchid after all.

But he *must* have known, anyway. In her letters, Emilie had spoken of a secret Grandfather knew. Spindrift had assumed it was the black orchid, and she couldn't say she knew it hadn't been without admitting she'd read more of the letters than she was supposed to. Luckily, keeping her mouth shut looked exactly the same as listening.

"I have feared this day," said Grandfather quietly. "Dreaded it." He folded his hands, unfolded them, rubbed them over his face. Spindrift watched his wrinkles stretch and settle back into their usual places as Grandfather's words sank in. Dreaded it? But why?

"Nonetheless, I was sure it would come, and so I was almost impatient for it. I admit, I didn't have to wait as long as I thought. Your mother was several years older," said Grandfather, looking right at Spindrift, "and I was several years older than that."

Clémence gasped so Spindrift didn't have to. "It was yours?" Spindrift asked.

"It is our family's," said Grandfather. "There are gaps in its history, times when it was lost or stolen or unused, but it always comes back to us. We always find it again because we must. I do not know what, exactly, inspires it to begin working one day when it didn't the day before. Perhaps it senses when its owner is ready, or when its owner is in need of it. What have you learned of its origins?"

"I know it's one of the Seven Sages. The seventh," said Spindrift.

"Good. The Sages all had families," said Grandfather, looking from Spindrift to Clémence to Max to see who would be the first one to piece it together. It was Max.

"Each orchid belongs to each family!" Max exclaimed, and Grandfather nodded approvingly.

"Exactly. Eleanor is our direct ancestor. Roland, whom you have unfortunately encountered"—he touched his wounded cheek—"is descended from Brand, the First Sage. He is, as he says, Son of the Red Orchid, as you, Spindrift, are the Daughter of the Black. This is why it is happy to serve you. It is as eager to make you happy as I am."

"Is that why it didn't work so well for me when I tried to make a wish?" asked Clémence.

Grandfather put down his teacup and spread his hands. "Yes and no. The Sages intended for the orchids to stay within their families, and those families have connections to them and to each other. Still, the Sages seemed to realize that occasionally families die out with no heirs, and so the orchid *will* work for another if it is given to them, and then for the descendants of the one it was given to. It will work if it is taken by force. This is the situation that every other orchid, apart from ours and Roland's, finds itself in now. None of them are owned by the families of the Sages anymore, as best as I have learned. What is fact is that the black orchid has been in our family since its creation, and what is fact is that this is a curse."

Spindrift's own teacup fell from her hand at the force of Grandfather's last word, splashing its contents on her lap and tumbling to the carpet. Grandfather, usually the first to jump up to fetch a cloth for such a spill, gestured to the others to ignore it. The room was silent other than the ticking clock on the wall, which waited for no one.

Curse, echoed Grandfather's voice in Spindrift's head.

"Yes," said Grandfather as if he'd heard it. "A curse. For some, you see, possessing one orchid isn't enough. There will always be people who, when given power, desire more of it." His voice shook. "This is why Roland wants your orchid. It seems, if he was not bluffing, that he has assembled almost the whole collection. The black orchid has been yours since the day you came to me because it was yours, given to you, and because it was safer that way. It may serve our family, yes, but we have a duty to protect it. I would never let it fall into another's hands. But I did not predict this, and I must protect *you*, my dearest. You have no idea how much I don't wish to do this, but you must give it back to me."

Spindrift jumped up from the couch, her hands clenched to fists. "What? Why?"

"Because I will not let you be hurt by it!" he said. Spindrift felt Clémence and Max staring at them, but she didn't turn her gaze from Grandfather. "Emilie went in search of the other orchids," he said, unaware that Spindrift had already guessed this from the letters she wasn't supposed to have read. "I even encouraged it.

They do not belong to the Sages' families, so why should they not belong to us? And it was the collecting itself that mattered, the finding of precious things. I don't think that in the beginning your mother had any desire for the kind of power uniting the orchids would bring her. I simply think she wanted to prove she could do it. She wanted to prove that to me.

"And so," said Grandfather, taking a deep breath, "just before your first birthday, she found a second one to keep the black orchid company. Shortly after, she located another, but she had begun to suspect that one of the members of her crew was not as loyal as she needed him to be. Roland was the *Masdevallia*'s quartermaster. I didn't find out until much later that his claim to the red orchid was a rightful one, but he didn't only want the red. Rather than let him get his hands on all of them, she gave him the red one, which wasn't enough. She hid the third and was, I believe, ready to put the black orchid somewhere for safekeeping when . . ."

He stopped. Spindrift waited, Clémence and Max, too, but he did not go on. His shoulders began to shake. He bowed his head, and sobs racked his body. Spindrift jumped up and ran to him, taking his hand in her own.

"The *Masdevallia* sank," she whispered, the man's earlier words coming back to her. She'd tried to block them out at the time. She still didn't want to think them now.

I killed your daughter.

"Sabotage," whispered Grandfather. "I do not know exactly how. I know she somehow managed to put you in a lifeboat and send you to shore, with a note for whoever found you and your crystal ball. The *Masdevallia* and all of its crew—or so I thought—sank without a trace."

"Someone else survived," said Clémence.

"Yes," said Grandfather, holding out a shaking hand. "The orchid, please, Spindrift."

Spindrift paced the floor of her room, which felt emptier without the orchid in it with her. Clémence and Max were asleep in the parlor and Grandfather had retired to bed, taking the crystal ball with him, though she wondered if he was having as much trouble sleeping as she was.

Never before had she felt and thought so many different things at once. It was exhausting, but not exhausting enough to make her climb under the covers and try to close her eyes.

Her parents hadn't died in a shipwreck caused by a storm. She'd known this to be true almost her entire life and now suddenly it wasn't. What else wasn't true? She took a few steps toward the window and reached out to touch the glass, feel its realness, cold and smooth.

Roland, the *Masdevallia*'s quartermaster, had killed Spindrift's mother and father because he wanted the orchids they were searching for. But if that was true, there must be a reason he hadn't waited for Emilie to find them all. He must have spent the years since trying to locate them, and now he had all but two of them in his possession. The black one was in Grandfather's room, and one unknown was out there somewhere but Roland knew where to find it.

And Grandfather had known about the orchids all along, let her have one as a plaything, safe while it refused to bloom. All this time, he'd never told her. Tears stung her eyes, and she blindly felt her way onto the window seat. Huge sobs burst from her, and she buried her face in her knees. Roland had killed her parents. The orchids had killed her parents with the obsession they created. Grandfather had known all of it but pretended not to, even when she'd told him about the customer asking for a black orchid that bloomed as you looked at it.

She gritted her teeth. It was *hers*, and Grandfather had taken it away now that the magic worked. It wasn't fair, and it scared her. Roland would stop at nothing to collect the orchids, like any ordinary orchid hunter gathering flowers that were still alive to bring himself wealth and fame. Grandfather was all she had left.

Angry as she was at him, she couldn't bear the thought of him being hurt, and neither of them was safe as long as Roland was out there, wanting the orchid she had.

Roland must be stopped.

She sat there for a long time, feeling her rage shift, inch by inch. Slowly, the sky over Lux began to lighten. The sun peeked over the horizon, and below her window, the wheels of the lamplighter's cart squeaked as he arrived to extinguish the flames.

Beyond her room, a door opened and closed. Spindrift crept out to find Grandfather in the kitchen, filling the kettle and putting dishes in their cupboards.

"Good morning, my dear," he said without turning around. "Would you like tea?"

"Yes, please," she answered.

"Did you sleep well?"

"Yes." The lie tasted like bad food on her tongue, but it wouldn't be the last one she'd tell him.

Finally, he turned so she could see his face, which looked as tired as she felt. "I am sorry I kept so much from you," he said. "It seemed the best thing to do at the time."

Without thinking, Spindrift ran across the tiles and threw her arms around him. He made a sound of surprise and hugged her in return, patting her back with one gentle hand. He felt so thin beneath his threadbare sweater, so old. So weak. He had triumphed over Roland the previous evening, in his shop surrounded by the helpful objects he knew so well, but Roland would try again.

"He said he knew where the last one was," she said, stepping back. "It can't be in Lux or he would have it already."

"I agree," said Grandfather, reaching for a lemon from a bowl and a sharp knife. "I imagine he will leave us alone for a while now; he'll make preparations to collect the other one before coming to claim ours." The blade in his hand slid too forcefully through the fruit. "Don't worry, Spindrift. He will not get it, and he will not hurt us."

Spindrift nodded as if she believed him.

"At any rate, we have time. Roland is a sailor. Wherever the last one is, he will go to it by ship. It may be months before he disturbs us again, so we will ready ourselves. Let me worry about that. You are a little girl and should be concerned with your final week of school, and your friends, and the holiday we shall all take together soon."

"Have you spoken to Maman and Papa?" Clémence asked from the doorway. Grandfather took down a third teacup and dropped a slice of lemon into it.

"I have. They shall miss you, of course, but I've assured them we won't be gone long. We shall leave the morning after your schooling finishes; they shall bring cases with your things on your last day."

"Where are we going?" asked Max from behind his sister. Grandfather got a fourth teacup and began to pour the tea, the scents of bergamot and lemon filling the kitchen.

"Fumus," he said. "I realize this may be a bit selfish, but I thought of all the places Spindrift should see, her father's home must be first."

A wide smile spread Spindrift's cheeks as her mind raced.

This was perfect.

"I'm glad you're so happy, *chérie*," said Grandfather at the sight. "A good choice, then. All right, all of you, drink your tea and get ready. I will put croissants on the table in a few minutes."

Max and Clémence returned to the parlor to find their shoes and socks, and Spindrift went to her room to change for school. When they'd eaten their fill of croissants and butter and preserves, they followed Grandfather down to the shop, Spindrift's heart sinking at the chaos there. A deep, dark anger bubbled in her stomach with her tea and breakfast.

"Would you like us to help?" asked Max.

"No, no," said Grandfather. "I will take care of it. Go and learn things."

Spindrift's bag felt lighter without the weight of the crystal ball inside, so used she'd become in such a short time to carrying it everywhere with her.

"Are you all right, Spin?" Clémence put her arm around Spindrift's shoulders as they walked down Nightbrick Lane. "It couldn't have been easy to hear all of that last night."

"I'm all right," she said, still thinking of her orchid. She would have it back soon. She *needed* it back, for even though she now had a wish it couldn't grant outright, it could help. So could Clémence and Max. "I need to talk to you both," she said, turning onto Argent Avenue and gazing at the river.

Yes, she had a wish.

She wanted revenge.

CHAPTER ELEVEN

Flight

IT WAS THE FINAL DAY of school. Madame Dulac had all but given up on making her charges concentrate on anything, and so all of Spindrift's lessons were a great deal noisier than usual. She, Clémence, and Max, however, were quieter, exchanging looks between themselves as the other students carried on around them.

In the courtyard after lunch, Tristan spotted Spindrift and started to walk over, presumably seizing his chance to be horrible to her one final time before he didn't see her again for weeks. Spindrift's fingers curled.

Enough. People like him grew up to be people like Roland, who didn't care who they hurt in their quests to get what they wanted. Tristan's steps faltered as she glared at him, but he came closer.

"You're horrible," she said before he could open his sneering mouth. "Nobody likes you because you're so horrible. Yes, my parents are dead, and it's very sad, but I didn't kill them, and even though they're dead I'm *still* not as lonely as you are. Perhaps if you were a little kinder to people, you wouldn't need to be nasty to me just so someone would actually speak to you for once. Go away. I'm not saying another word to you ever again."

Behind her shoulder, Max choked. Tristan's eyes widened and his mouth opened and closed like a fish. Spindrift grabbed Clémence's hand and turned on her heel, leading Clémence and Max away to a far corner.

"Wow, Spin, remind me never to make you cross," said Clémence.

"He deserved it," said Spindrift. She chanced a look in Tristan's direction. He was standing alone by the school door, staring down at his shoes.

"He did," Max agreed.

Clémence glanced around to make sure no one was listening and lowered her voice to a whisper. "Are we ready?"

"We will be," said Spindrift. "We have your cases and I'll pack mine when we go home." Grandfather was busy at this moment preparing to close the shop for two weeks, moving some of the more precious contents up to the apartment and making a pile in the parlor of things they would need to take with them. Spindrift had looked it over before breakfast that morning, checking the pairs of wings each of them would wear for the journey to their destination and leafing through Grandfather's book of maps. She'd picked up a compass, watching both of its needles move back and forth until one pointed north, the other toward the place the holder wanted to go. She'd smiled as she'd remembered the customer returning it, claiming it didn't work. Grandfather said it did, and she trusted him far more than some grumpy old lady.

The afternoon dragged, the lessons useless. Spindrift spent the time alternating between making a list inside her head of the things she needed to take with her that Grandfather hadn't already gathered and glancing out the window for the shadow of a man in a black cloak. He wasn't really out there. He would be preparing to sail off to find the final orchid, or already on his ship.

Still, Spindrift worried about Grandfather alone in the shop, the door unlocked for customers. The slight knot in her stomach tightened a little bit more.

Finally, the last lesson ended, with none of them having learned a single thing, and Madame Dulac walked

through the hallways ringing her bell. Spindrift, Max, and
Clémence were among the first outside, bursting through
the gates into the bright sunshine of Magothire Street.
Though she was eager to get home and make preparations,
Spindrift walked slowly, peering in each of the windows
and turning her eyes skyward to see the silver- and gold-
leafed trees.

Max nudged her with his elbow. "We're coming back,"
he said softly. Clémence was up ahead, her face pressed to
a hothouse's green-tinted window.

"I know," said Spindrift. All her life, she'd thought of
the ocean as her home, and Lux simply the place she lived.
On the eve of her first time leaving it, she was surprised at
how much she was going to miss the city.

But, as Max said, they'd be back. Together they swept
up Clémence and made their way down Argent Avenue
and up Nightbrick Lane, the door of the shop soon coming
into view. Every day since Roland's visit here she'd held her
breath as she opened the door, hoping he hadn't returned.

The shop looked entirely normal, if a bit empty, its
glass cases cleared of their valuables. Grandfather was in
the back room, on the top rung of a ladder, placing a book
into its place among fifty others. Spindrift went swiftly to
a shelf and then joined Max and Clémence at the bottom
of the ladder.

"Hello, you three!" he said. "Well, the eve is upon us! Let me finish up here and I'll come upstairs. There's some food that needs eating before we leave." Grandfather turned his eyes back to the books and, unseen, Spindrift nodded at Max.

"Wait," said Max. "I was wondering if you'd tell me about that book." Max craned his neck to read the spine of one several inches to Grandfather's left.

Grandfather would always, always discuss the treasures in his shop. "This one?" he asked, fingertips searching it out. "Oh, let me tell you about this one. . . ."

Spindrift tugged on Clémence's hand and led her up the stairs to the apartment. Grandfather probably hadn't even noticed them leave. Tiptoeing, so their footsteps wouldn't give them away below, they went down the corridor and stopped outside Grandfather's bedroom.

"Are you sure about this?" Clémence asked. "I mean, you're right, Spin, about all of it, but Monsieur Morel is going to be so angry when he finds out."

"This won't be what makes him angriest," said Spindrift, turning the handle. "And we need it."

"I know." Clémence nodded, though she still looked doubtful. She never liked getting in trouble, although she was always more than up for a little mischief if she was sure she wouldn't get caught. This time the discovery would happen sooner rather than later.

"Help me look."

Grandfather's room was small and neat and without anything unnecessary, much like the man who slept in it. There weren't very many places to hide something, but Grandfather had been counting on Spindrift's goodness to stop her from looking.

She was still good. He didn't know it yet, but she was doing this to protect him.

Mostly.

"All of his socks have holes," said Clémence, closing the drawer that held them. "Why doesn't he get them mended, or buy new ones?"

"He forgets, I think," said Spindrift. "He never seems to want anything new for himself. For the shop, yes, and for me, but never for him. Even with things he might need, he just doesn't think about it."

"Are you sure we shouldn't tell him?" Clémence stopped searching and faced Spindrift, a worried expression on her face. "He might come with us."

"He wouldn't. He thinks he's keeping me safe by keeping me here, but we won't be safe until I stop Roland, and Roland killed my parents—he doesn't even deserve one orchid, let alone all of them."

"That's true," said Clémence. "I can't even imagine, Spin, how horrible it must be to know they didn't die in a storm. How horrible it must be to not have them at all."

"It's all right," said Spindrift. It wasn't, but there was nothing else to say. She opened the cabinet beside Grandfather's bed, and a tightness in her chest released at the sight of the crystal ball on a bed of folded silk. A scarf, or some such. Quickly, she swapped the orchid for the crystal ball she'd taken from the shop a few moments before. It wasn't exactly the same, the borrowed one a tiny bit bigger, and of course it wouldn't do the same thing, but if Grandfather opened the cabinet later to check the orchid was safe, it might fool him for just long enough.

Wishes would come later. For now she simply needed to have it.

She and Clémence were in the parlor when Max and Grandfather came upstairs, still talking about the book. Spindrift couldn't remember the last time she'd heard Max talk so much at once; perhaps he was as interested in the book as he'd pretended to be. He glanced over at Spindrift, who nodded almost imperceptibly.

The hours went nearly as slowly as they had at school, made all the more difficult by the need to act normal so Grandfather wouldn't suspect. Over dinner he told them what he knew of Fumus, a place he'd been only once, and they feigned excitement at the places Grandfather thought they'd soon be seeing with their own eyes.

When dessert had settled as much as it was going to in Spindrift's topsy-turvy stomach, she went to her room to pack her warmest clothes on top of the crystal ball at the bottom of her bag. She watered the real black orchid that she'd purchased from the hothouse, hoping that when Grandfather stopped being angry at her—if he ever did—he would do so again while she was away.

Voices came from the parlor, Clémence and Grandfather talking while Max likely sat in silence. Spindrift knew Clémence wasn't as sure of this plan as Spindrift herself, or even Max, but she was a good friend, Spindrift's very best friend, and so she was coming anyway. Spindrift had been right in what she'd said to Tristan that afternoon; she wasn't alone. A warm feeling filled her chest. When all this was over, she would have to think of a way to thank Clémence and Max for their help, because although she would never admit it to them, she'd be far too afraid to do this alone. Even Emilie hadn't sailed off on the *Masdevallia* by herself; she'd had Spindrift's father and a whole ship's crew with her.

A crew that had included Roland. Spindrift shoved the last of her clothes into her case, making sure to leave room in the top for one last thing.

"All ready?" Grandfather asked when she arrived in the parlor, dragging the heavy bag behind her. She nodded, and Max, curled in the corner of the couch, frowned.

"Monsieur Morel?"

"Yes, Maximilian?"

"How are we supposed to carry our things while we're flying? We can't wear our bags on our backs. The wings are in the way."

"Aha." Grandfather stood and went over to the pile of luggage and assorted items by the window and took from the table there a locket, which was a strange thing to be needing on a holiday. Spindrift had never seen it before; certainly Grandfather had never worn it. His wrinkled but still nimble fingers released the clasp and it opened, four windows unfolding from what had been a silver square. "Yours first, Max," he said with a smile, hoisting Max's case and holding it above the locket. Spindrift, Max, and Clémence watched openmouthed as Max's case shrank down, down, down until it flattened and slotted neatly into one of the windows. It possibly wasn't the cleverest piece of magic Spindrift had ever seen one of his objects perform, but it was quite good. He placed Clémence's into the next, then reached for Spindrift's bag. She bit her tongue against her protest— she was not, in fact, completely ready—and watched it almost disappear. Grandfather's own bag contained few clothes, as he always wore the same things, and was mostly full of the books, compass, binoculars, and other assorted trinkets he'd decided were important.

"Oooh, is it heavy now?" asked Clémence. Grandfather held out the locket to her and she hung it around her neck. "It hardly weighs anything!"

"Does that answer your question, Max? Good. Clémence, it suits you. Would you like to be the guardian of our belongings?"

Clémence nodded, inspecting the engravings on the locket's surface. Spindrift breathed a sigh of relief.

"Excellent. Now. As it isn't a school night, a treat before bed, I think. We must wake up early, but not too early." He left for the kitchen, Spindrift's heart feeling as if it were being clenched by a fist. Oh, she hoped he wouldn't be too angry with her.

Over thick, dark hot chocolate and delicate, crumbly macarons, Grandfather taught the three of them to play cards, betting with matches from a box kept on the mantel above the empty hearth. Spindrift couldn't concentrate and kept asking him to explain the rules again. At the end of the evening, Max, who'd barely said a word for an hour, had the biggest pile of matchsticks in front of him.

"Well done, Max," said Grandfather. "Do you know, I

think you've won enough to trade them for that book you found so fascinating, if you wish."

A wide smile broke across Max's face, his bright teeth glowing in the light from the alchemist's lamps. "Really?"

"Really," said Grandfather. "I'll go fetch it. Spindrift, will you get the pillows and blankets to make them comfortable for the night."

"Yes, Grandfather." The bedding was kept in a chest along the wall. Clémence joined Spindrift there, helping her and leaning down to whisper in Spindrift's ear.

"Do we have everything?"

Spindrift shook her head. "There's one more thing I need."

Grandfather returned with the book and handed it to Max. "Right," he said. "Get some rest, all of you, and tomorrow we shall be off on a great adventure!"

Max, Clémence, and Spindrift all exchanged looks. "Good night, Monsieur Morel," said the twins together. Spindrift said nothing, instead following Grandfather out into the hallway.

"Good night," she said, trying to keep her voice steady. Grandfather placed his hands on her shoulders and gazed at her for a long, searching moment.

"The sweetest dreams, my dearest," he said. "Tomorrow you will fly over the ocean from which you came to me."

A lump formed in the back of Spindrift's throat; she could only nod. He kissed her forehead and released her, leaving her standing there trembling with fear and sorrow and excitement. It took some time before she managed to force her feet to move to her own room, going about her usual routine so that he'd hear her getting ready for sleep if he chose to listen.

They'd agreed they would sleep beforehand, and rest came much more easily than Spindrift thought it might, pulling her under in moments. She awoke with a start, for an instant unsure where she was, though that was ridiculous. Not since she was a baby had she woken up anywhere but in this room. Then she feared she'd overslept and Grandfather would be in the kitchen, making tea and breakfast to fuel their journey to Fumus.

But no. It was still dark outside. By the moonlight coming in through the window, she dressed in the clothes she'd left herself, took a small brass key from the cabinet beside her bed, and found a quill and a piece of paper in her discarded schoolbag.

The day before, leafing through Grandfather's book of maps, she'd memorized what she needed to know, repeating it to herself over and over on the walk to school. Now she let the quill ink out the unfamiliar letters and numbers at the top of the page.

N 48°51'24", E 2°21'03"
21st day of the Month of Illumination, in the Year
of the Ancients

Dearest Grandfather,
I know when you wake up and find us gone, you
will be terribly angry with me. I'm sorry, truly
I am, but if we have a duty to the black orchid,
we must protect her. I have to stop Roland, and I
know you'd never let me go if you knew, and you
definitely wouldn't come with me. You've never
liked boats or the water, but they are my home. I
will be all right, and Max and Clémence are com-
ing along to help. As soon as we stop him, we'll
come home.

I have taken Maman's letters. I promise you I'll
keep them safe and not spill tea on them, but some-
where in them is a clue about where she hid the last
orchid he's looking for. If we're going to get there
first, we need to know where it is.

I love you more than anything. You are my
family, and so is the black orchid, and I have to
protect you both.

Love,
Spindrift

There. She was coming back. Of course she was, but just in case . . . Grandfather would have a letter to keep in a wooden box, just as he had with her mother's. She folded it in three and silently slipped through the door, out into the hallway, and down to the parlor.

Clémence was snoring. Spindrift stifled a giggle and shook her awake, then Max. Both of them blinked in the darkness, grumbling and trying to turn over under their blankets, but Spindrift persisted. "Wake up," she whispered. "It's time to go."

Max sat bolt upright, memory seeping through the heavy haze of sleep. "Oh," he whispered. "Oh! Wake up, Clém."

Sure it was safe to leave them, Spindrift crept over to a bookshelf, where the wooden box of her mother's letters had sat neglected for a week. Ever since the night Roland had come and Grandfather had made Spindrift give him the orchid, he hadn't suggested reading them in the evenings, and neither had she. It had been better for him to think that she didn't want to.

"Clémence, I need the locket," she said. Half asleep, Clémence stumbled over, banging her toe against a table leg and yelping loudly. All three of them held their breath, exchanging panicked stares until enough time passed that Spindrift was sure Grandfather hadn't been disturbed.

From the locket, Clémence pulled Spindrift's case. They watched it grow in just the opposite way than it had shrunk until it was its proper size and Clémence struggled to hold it. Spindrift took it from her and reached deep inside, grasping the orchid's crystal ball from the very bottom and pulling it free. Then she placed the wooden box on top of her clothes and closed the bag tight. Back into the locket it went. Next, Spindrift took Grandfather's bag and helped herself to the compass, the only other thing she'd need for now. She was about to close the locket again when Max stopped her and removed his own bag so that he could put the book from Grandfather into it.

Now they were ready. Over their clothes they donned heavy cloaks to protect them from the wind as they flew. Each one chose their wings: red and gold for Clémence, blue for Max, and the black of a raven's wing for Spindrift. The final pair, a silvery white, looked sad and lonely on the floor. Spindrift quickly placed her letter on the table nearby and turned away so she wouldn't have to see them.

Every sound they made as they inched toward the stairs to the shop echoed through the apartment loud as a siren. She was positive Grandfather would wake up and stop them at the last minute, and she waited for a second on each stair for the inevitable voice to come.

But it didn't come. Down in the shop it was safer to make a little more noise while they wrestled and buckled themselves into the magnificent wings that spread two feet out from each of their shoulders.

Spindrift patted the pocket in her cloak to make sure she still had the orchid and the compass, one object smooth, the other hard-edged and sharp.

It was the height of summer, but the shadows of Nightbrick Lane were cold so early in the morning, and the cobblestones slick with dew. This time Spindrift didn't wish them dry with Orchid's help; their feet wouldn't be touching them for more than another moment.

"I'm sorry," she whispered as she closed the door behind them. She stood, staring at it, until Max touched her hand.

"Are we going?" he asked.

Yes. Yes, they were going.

The wings flapped, strong enough to carry grown men across the earth. Spindrift felt weightless, rising past her bedroom window and over the roof. The Arch of the Seventh Sage, *her* sage, came into view atop Sages' Hill. It was a sign.

"Where do we go?" asked Clémence. Carefully, Spindrift reached into her pocket and removed the compass, gripping it tight in her hand so she didn't drop it to the ground far below, where it would shatter into a thousand useless pieces.

Work, she pleaded inside her head. *Please work*.

The needles spun, one settling with its arrow below the large, engraved *N* on the rim around the glass. The other whirled back and forth. Spindrift concentrated, thinking of exactly what she wanted.

The needle stopped. "That way," she said, pointing.

Soon the city was gone and below their feet was a patchwork of fields, turned a hundred shades of green by the Month of Rains.

"How far is it?" yelled Max.

"I don't know!" Spindrift yelled back. Clémence was too busy enjoying herself to speak at all, turning somersaults in the air and laughing into the wind. The sun rose higher and higher above them, warming Spindrift's chilled bones. This wouldn't have been her wish the way it was Clémence's, but it *was* fun. She looked from side to side, first at Clémence and then at Max, grinning in challenge.

The race was on.

Faster and faster they sped through the sky until Spindrift was half blinded by the wind and gasping for breath as she yelled for them to stop. Twenty yards ahead, Clémence slowed to an easy drift, laughing. Nearby, Max caught Spindrift's eyes and rolled his own.

Water shimmered in the distance, a narrow channel dividing one land from another. The wind dropped, and so did Spindrift, Max, and Clémence. Only a few feet, just enough to make all three of them scream. Gently, the air currents guided them down and deposited them at the water's edge on a barren stretch of coastline.

Here?

But...

Spindrift fell to her knees on the muddy shore. They'd been so close to home when they sank, so nearly safe. They were as close to Lux as it was possible to get by sea. Another day—perhaps mere hours—and Spindrift might still have her parents.

"We didn't have to fly very long, did we?" asked Max softly, putting his small brown hand on Spindrift's trembling shoulder. "I'm sorry, Spin."

"It's okay." She wiped her eyes and pushed herself to her feet, stumbling a little because of the uneven ground and the weight of the bag on her chest. "I'm all right."

"You sure, Spin?" asked Clémence.

"I'm sure." Spindrift opened the bag and reached to the bottom for Orchid. "Orchid," she said.

The flower bloomed and wavered in the air above the water. "Spindrift! How nice to see you again," said Orchid. "Do you have a wish?"

"Yes." Spindrift swallowed hard and stared out at the vast expanse of steely gray water.

It was out there. A ship was an object, wasn't it? An object made of objects.

She swallowed again. Orchid hovered, her dress shifting with the wind.

"I wish for you to raise the *Masdevallia*."

CHAPTER TWELVE

The Masdevallia

NOTHING HAPPENED. SPINDRIFT COULDN'T SEE where her mistake had been. "Um. I wish . . ."

Orchid held up one of her elegant, long-fingered hands. The ground rumbled. A roaring, rushing sound swelled louder and louder.

On the surface of the water, a wave began to build.

"Get back!" shouted Clémence, grabbing her brother's arm and Spindrift's hand, yanking them away from the edge. They scrambled over shifting dunes, ducking down and covering their ears. Spindrift felt the world shake all the way down to her teeth. She closed her eyes and waited for it to fade away.

Finally, it did. She dropped her hands and heard

shouting in the distance. She stood, searching. At the opposite end of the nearest field, a man was pointing toward the water.

Spindrift turned. Clémence and Max rose to stand beside her, and all the three could do was stand agape at the sight. Not entirely in a good way.

"I didn't really think about what it would look like after ten years in the water," said Spindrift after a while.

"Is that a fish in that basket thing at the top?" Clémence wrinkled her nose.

Spindrift picked the crystal ball up off the sand. "Orchid?"

She bloomed again. "Yes?"

"Could you, um . . ." Spindrift pointed at the battered, seaweed-strewn hulk. "Could you possibly fix that? I wish for you to fix it."

It happened almost instantly, and there, to the gasps of Spindrift, Clémence, and Max, was the *Masdevallia* in all her glory, beautiful as she had ever been.

Spindrift could barely breathe.

"Wow," said Clémence, which about covered it. "It's enormous."

It was, indeed, enormous. The *Masdevallia* bobbed on the water, towering over them even from this distance. Her hull gleamed, and her sails billowed. From atop one of several masts, a flag flew, emblazoned with a black flower.

Spindrift yanked the lever on her wings and took off, Clémence squealing in surprise from the ground behind her. She beat them to the ship by several seconds, landing on the slick deck, which was polished to such a high shine Spindrift saw her own face reflected back in it.

The outside of the ship was painted black, but everything else was gleaming wood and crisp white sails. It all felt . . . familiar, somehow. Warm, friendly.

She belonged here. She'd started her life here.

Two *thump*s sounded behind her. "Spin!" said Clémence.

"Leave her," Max whispered. Spindrift's eyes ached with the effort of trying to see everything at once, the masts and sails, bowsprit and crow's nest, the latter now empty of any and all fish. Somehow she knew the names of these things, as if they were the first words she'd ever learned.

Maybe they were.

Slowly, she edged over to the railing and looked down at the water's surface. She kept her hand on the wood as she walked around the entire deck, ending up where she'd started.

Alone—and she was glad Max had held Clémence back—she descended into the depths of the ship. Here, too, everything was wood or white. In a large room, hammocks hung from the ceiling, still now, but when the ship was moving they would rock their inhabitants to sleep in time with the waves.

She turned a doorknob, and her breath caught in her chest. Here was a large bed, a porthole above the pillows. A clock hung on the wall. This was where her parents would have slept. She pulled off her wings and sat down on the edge of the bed, staring at her knees.

Almost an hour later, according to the clock, Clémence and Max came to find her. "Spin?" Clémence said softly. "We're sorry. I mean, we know this is probably difficult, but those people are shouting at us from the shore. They're very curious."

"I think perhaps we'd better go," said Max.

Spindrift nodded. "Orchid," she said, grasping the crystal ball and waiting for the flower to bloom. "I wish for the *Masdevallia* to set sail for open water. Quickly." They had to catch up to Roland.

The ship began to move. Together, Spindrift, Clémence, and Max ran back up to the deck to watch the land slide past. Spindrift asked Clémence for Grandfather's case from the locket and took from it the binoculars she'd seen there. She looked through them at the curious people on land, their expressions that of rather satisfying confusion. Let them have fun guessing what had happened here.

It was as windy on the deck as it had been in the air, so soon they retreated down below, leaving the *Masdevallia* to sail itself. Clémence removed all the bags from the locket and placed them in a spare hammock. Max surveyed them and frowned.

"Um. We didn't bring any food," he said.

That was true, but it didn't matter. "What would you like to eat?" asked Spindrift, raising the crystal ball.

"Anything?"

"Anything," she assured him, hoping that was right. Orchid had never placed any limitations on food, provided Spindrift didn't wish for something that was still alive. Spindrift had never much liked oysters, anyway.

"I want a chocolate cake," said Max.

"And I want that lobster thing Monsieur Morel makes. With the sauce," said Clémence.

Spindrift eyed them both. "For breakfast?"

"Yes," they said.

"All right," said Spindrift, summoning the orchid to wish for the food and adding a plate of croissants for herself. Max found knives and forks in a drawer, and napkins, too. They sat down at the polished table in the galley to eat, their plates sliding a little with the rhythm of the fast-moving ship. Thirsty, Spindrift wished for water with elderflowers, the taste making her heart pang for Grandfather's table below the magnificent chandelier. He'd be awake by now, almost certainly.

She pushed her half-eaten food away.

"So, how do we find the last orchid?" Clémence finished chewing a mouthful of lobster and washed it down with a swig from her glass. "Can you use that compass thing?"

Spindrift hadn't thought of that. She fetched it from where she'd left it on her parents' bed and concentrated, watching the needles swing. As before, one settled on *N* very quickly, but the other wouldn't stop spinning no matter how hard she thought of where she wanted to go.

The trouble was she didn't know exactly where she wanted to go, or even which orchid she was searching for. Though the *Masdevallia* had been closer to her home in Lux than she'd ever imagined, she'd nonetheless known roughly where it lay all those years, and she knew its name. Without detail, the compass was useless.

She would have to use the letters, as she'd suspected. Mindful of the promise she'd made to Grandfather that he must have read by now, she waited for Max and Clémence to finish eating and wished the table clear before she took the wooden box from her bag. The brass key from her bedside cabinet fit perfectly into the lock, and she opened the lid, ready to reach for one of her mother's letters.

A new envelope rested on top of the others, laid flat so Spindrift could see her own name scrawled across it. Max and Clémence watched her as she slowly removed the letter; she could feel the weight of their eyes.

20th day of the Month of Illumination, in the Year
of the Ancients
N 48°51'24", E 2°21'03"

My dearest Spindrift,
If you are reading this, you have done exactly what
I feared you would do and are now on your way,
sailing aboard the Masdevallia. *I had hoped that I*
was wrong, that your behavior these past days didn't
mean what I thought it meant, but clearly it did.

I am furious with you, chérie, *and heart-*
broken, too. However, those are matters that can
be addressed later, for my anguish means nothing
compared to your safety. If you are wondering why
I didn't stop you when I suspected, that is the rea-
son. I felt forbidding you would only make you
more determined to go, and I was right, though
that is little comfort now. That determination
might have made you reckless, forced you to leave

alone or without the supplies you needed. Even as I wished I was wrong, I prepared you as best I could.

Regardless, there are things you must know and things you must do. First, you are clever and resourceful, my dear, more so than you think you are. Second, you must protect yourself. Make whatever wishes you must in order to keep yourself—and Max and Clémence, too, whose parents think we are all on a trip to Fumus—safe and well. The orchid cannot change you, but it can change the ship. Remember that.

Finally, and perhaps most importantly, you must read all of Emilie's letters to try to discover where she left the final orchid, but hints as to its location, if indeed there are any, are not the only information they contain.

I always meant to be by your side when you read these, to answer your questions and soothe your fears. I worry now that you will believe everything you read, and your impression of your parents will sour. I can say only that they were controlled by a force you cannot imagine, a force you MUST RESIST. The obsession overtook them both, your mother in particular. It is not who they truly were. They made mistakes, as did I.

Please, Spindrift, do not judge them, or me, too harshly.

Love,

Grandfather

Spindrift read Grandfather's letter over and over, her eyes catching each time on the words *MUST RESIST*, heavier and darker than all the ones around them, like he'd traced them again and again with a quill until its point was in danger of piercing the sheet of paper. When it was so burned into her mind that she felt she could recite it from memory, she passed it to Clémence, who read it with Max leaning over her shoulder.

"Orchid," called Spindrift, her hand on the crystal.

The orchid appeared above the table. "Yes?"

Spindrift thought of what Grandfather had said. In a way, the ship was like the orchid herself, an object with something, or things, living inside it. And Orchid had been able to grant Spindrift's wish to hear her from within the ball.

That felt so long ago. Her wishes from that day seemed so silly now, so small.

"I wish for you to make the *Masdevallia* impossible to find," she said.

Orchid nodded. "It is so," she said. "But with limitations.

I warn you, Spindrift, that you aren't protected if you leave the ship; nor will you be able to see it if you aren't on it, unless you change your wish. There may also be magics that can get through my defenses."

"Thank you." Spindrift turned her attention back to the box of letters. The scrap of red card that Grandfather had used to mark their place was still there, though Spindrift had read several that were sent much later.

Part of her wanted to begin reading them in order, the way she and Grandfather had, and go through them slowly, methodically, savoring every word.

But there wasn't time. Roland was likely already ahead of them, racing toward the orchid Emilie had hidden. And he knew where it was, or so he claimed. There was no time to waste.

"He knew," said Clémence, sounding awed. Spindrift busied herself searching for the letter in which Emilie had written of the red orchid, her eyes firmly fixed on her hands feeling for an envelope thinner than the rest, just a scrap of paper within.

"He's angry with me," said Spindrift softly. She'd known he would be, but it was real now.

"It'll be all right, Spin," said Max. "People forgive each other. He will understand. We're here. We have to do this now."

Spindrift straightened her shoulders. Yes. Max was right. She wasn't going to just sit on this ship, bobbing in the middle of the ocean, doing nothing while Roland got the orchid and Grandfather paced the floor of the shop. She grasped a letter and pulled it out with such force that another came with it. One of them was very thin— hopefully the one she wanted—the other a more normal thickness of a sheet of paper folded in three.

23rd day of the Month of Illumination, in the Year
of the Stars
N 5°19'0", W 4°2'0"

Dearest Papa,
We are getting closer. I can feel it. Theo says I
shouldn't get my hopes up, but he is secretly as impa-
tient as I am to find one. How we will make it ours
when we do depends on the circumstances—there is
a cache of gold secreted away in case it is as easy as
purchasing it from its owner, though I think we are
all prepared for it to be more complicated than that.
My blades are sharp and my determination is
iron. Another orchid will be mine.
Love,
Emilie

Spindrift frowned. Her mother had been prepared to kill for an orchid. Had she needed to, in the end?

"I have an idea," said Max. "Spin, can you wish us a big map? And some pins."

"Of where?"

"Everywhere."

"Um. All right?" She called up Orchid and made the wish, passing the objects to Max as soon as they appeared in her hands. He went to the nearest wall and tacked the map up in the space between two portholes, then reached for the letter Spindrift had just placed on the table. Tapping his lips with his fingertip, he stood for a long time in front of the map before finally placing a silver pin in the middle of it.

1st day of the Month of Endless Fire, in the Year of the Stars
S 18°09', E 49°25'

Dearest Papa,
We found one. The red one. It works, though not as well as the black does for me, which is no great surprise. I do not have the same connection to the red, and still it does my bidding within its limitations. Those limitations both fascinate and frustrate me; I

must see how far I may push them. I tried with this
one simply to wish for all the others, and of course it
didn't work. I must seek them out myself.

   Love,

   Emilie

It was the right letter. She'd already seen this one and
only skimmed it, then placed it in Clémence's eagerly
grasping hands. They formed a sort of mechanism like
some of Grandfather's objects had, with Spindrift pluck-
ing a letter to read, then giving it to Clémence, who gave
it to Max, so he could mark on the map the coordinates
from which it was sent.

It was too much to hope for that Emilie had found
a third orchid, the one she'd hidden, so soon after finding the second one, and thus the next handful of letters
held no new information. Spindrift lingered over them
anyway, absorbing each word, trying to feel what her
mother had felt when she wrote them. Emilie might
have been sitting at this very table, dipping her quill into
an inkwell right where the box now sat. Perhaps she had
stayed up late to write to Grandfather, candles burning while the rest of the crew slept in their hammocks.
Perhaps her eyes had grown heavy and she'd yawned a
big, face-aching yawn.

A nap seemed in order; they really had woken very early. Spindrift looked to the others for agreement, and the twins nodded gratefully. They each picked a hammock and climbed in.

"You don't want to sleep in the big bed?" Clémence asked. Spindrift tried to peek over the edge of her hammock, but it tipped dangerously. She caught only the briefest glimpse of a Clémence-shaped parcel hanging nearby.

"No," said Spindrift, giving up and lying back to wait for the hammock to still as much as it would. Sleeping there didn't feel right somehow.

Twilight seeped in through the edges of the porthole, not quite full darkness but that magical blue hour that, in Lux, would have signaled the creaking of the lamplighter's cart. Clémence was snoring again. As gracefully as possible, which wasn't gracefully at all, Spindrift climbed from her bed and went up onto the deck.

A bitter wind blew, whipping her hair into her face and ripping tears from her eyes. She wiped them away, squinting, but there were no signs of light or land anywhere. The weight of the endless sky settled around her shoulders; the ocean was enormous. Never before had Spindrift felt so very small.

Down below once more, Spindrift found her orchid

and wished for alchemists' lamps. The galley bloomed with light, and she picked one up, carrying it to her parents' chamber. She wouldn't sleep here, but she would sit on the bed and think of her parents sailing off across the world in search of more objects like the one Spindrift held in her hand.

This was who they had been: sailors, orchid hunters of a very special kind, a daughter, a son, parents themselves after a while. Wrapped in the safety of their ship, Spindrift knew them both more and less than ever.

After a while, her thoughts turned outward, and she cast her eyes around the room. Cupboards lined the walls, places for her parents to have stored their belongings so that they wouldn't fall on them no matter how badly the ship pitched from side to side in bad weather.

Spindrift's eyes narrowed. Was anything in there? When Orchid had fixed the *Masdevallia*, had she fixed everything that belonged on it? There were plates and goblets and hammocks, after all.

The scent that burst from the first cupboard when she opened it nearly knocked her backward onto the bed. Not because it was unpleasant, no, but because . . .

She remembered. The cupboard was full of Emilie's clothes, and something deep inside Spindrift knew this perfume, lemons and cedar and something that made her think of the way clouds must smell. She buried her face in the first of the hanging dresses as she must have buried it into her mother's shoulder when she was small enough to be held.

She wasn't crying. No. Her eyes were still watering from the wind on the deck.

The next cupboard held her father's things, and these, too, called forth something old and necessary within her. He'd smelled like woodsmoke and pepper and black tea. She might not have Grandfather's nose, but these things she knew.

The next cupboard held a collection of books on several shelves and a wooden box on the lowest, down near Spindrift's knees. She pulled it out, nearly dropping it as recognition hit her.

She knew this box. It, or one exactly like it, was still sitting out on the long table in the galley. Without even bothering to close the cupboard door, she ran out to the table, fingers searching under a pile of letters for a small brass key.

It fit. The hinges opened smoothly, and inside was, somehow, exactly what she thought might be there, a row of envelopes pressed out from the tiny squares they'd once been folded into.

Spindrift pulled out the first one. The paper was thin, the handwriting familiar.

*15th day of the Month of Origins, in the Year of the
Wind
N 48°51'24", E 2°21'03"*

My dearest Emilie, it began.

CHAPTER THIRTEEN
Grandfather

15th day of the Month of Origins, in the Year of the Wind
N 48°51'24", E 2°21'03"

My dearest Emilie,
Oh, it is so hard to see you leave, though of course you must go. You are right that I won't come to visit you on the Masdevallia. *My own seafaring days are over, never to return.*

I find myself torn, for I know both the thrill and the danger of the adventure on which you're about to embark. I've done the best I could do to prepare you and to make you stronger than I was myself. As

*worried as I am, I wish more than anything for you
to succeed where I failed so spectacularly. It is your
destiny, our family's destiny, to unite them—of this
I am certain.*

Good luck. My very best to Theo.

Love,

Papa

"What does he mean?" asked Clémence, reading over the letter. "What does any of this mean?"

"I don't know," said Spindrift, "but they must be in pairs. For every letter she wrote, there should be an answer from him. He'd never have ignored one. Help me."

Max stood by the map as Spindrift and Clémence emptied the boxes and pulled the notes from their envelopes, discarding the latter on a corner of the table. All hope of keeping the letters in perfect order was abandoned. Every one of Grandfather's letters had been sent from Lux, and Max marked all the places from which Emilie had sent hers. A string of silver pins on the map, carving a path across the seas.

"Those ones don't matter," said Clémence, pointing to a pile. "They were all sent before she found the second orchid, the red one. We're looking for the third."

She was right. What mattered was where the ship had

been in the nine months between the discovery of the red orchid and the sinking of the *Masdevallia*, which Spindrift now knew hadn't been because of a storm.

Vengeance rose within her again. Roland had killed her parents just to try to get his hands on the black orchid! What would he do to obtain the last one?

There were still another fifty letters to read. Spindrift's eyes ached, and everywhere she looked she saw glowing dots burned into her vision by the lamps. Bracing herself against the rocking of the ship, she climbed to the deck to gulp the fresh air, stained with salt and chill.

The darkness was absolute until her gaze reached the sky, where the stars shone like the pins in the map. The railing around the deck was freezing cold and smooth under her hands. The mist from the waves after which her father had nicknamed her sprayed up onto her face. She wondered if Grandfather was all right without her.

They were far from land now, free of the channel in which the *Masdevallia* had rested, rotting, for so long.

"Spin?"

Clémence's call was nearly lost to the wind. "Yes?" shouted Spindrift.

"We're hungry!"

"Oh." She ran back to the top of the stairs and followed Clémence down. In the galley it was quiet enough to speak normally.

"I tried it," said Clémence, "you know, just to see."

The glass ball lay on the table, nestled in a mass of wadded cotton so it didn't roll away. Irritation sparked inside Spindrift like a popping candle flame. How dare Clémence touch it! It was hers!

Spindrift took a deep breath, shoving the annoyance away. She probably would have done the same thing. "What would you like to eat?"

"Ice cream," said Clémence.

"And meringues," added Max.

"Chocolate."

"Monsieur Morel's roast chicken."

Spindrift could barely keep up with the wishes, let alone Orchid, but she gave them everything they asked for. After all, they had come with her, and she could imagine how lonely this journey would be without them. A feast spread over the table, full of sugary delights that would be surely rationed at home. But they weren't at home, and there were no grown-ups to tell them what to do, so there was nothing for it but to eat themselves silly. Second and third helpings of everything. So full she might burst, Spindrift lay back on one of the long benches, groaning.

"I think I might be sick," said Max.

"Well, don't be," said Spindrift, forcing herself back up again and wishing the messy plates away. "We need to keep looking at the letters."

Spindrift skimmed her eyes over the dates with their funny numbers beneath. She'd come back and read all their contents later; right now they had to tell Orchid which way to steer the ship.

Four more letters from the Month of Endless Fire. No. Three from the Month of Feasts. Six from the Month of Souls, another five from the Month of Eternity.

It must be one of the next ones. Now she began to properly read again. And there it was, in the second letter Emilie had sent in the final month of the Year of the Stars.

11th day of the Month of Endings, in the Year of the Stars
S 26°38'45", E 15°9'14"

Dearest Papa,
Four years to find the second, four months to find the third. I believe they call to each other somehow, as if they are meant to be united.

I know now that they are meant to be mine. Why else would both the black and red bloom for me? And now the blue as well. They want me to possess them, all of them. I cannot stop. I must complete the collection, however long it takes me. Already I feel indescribable power, and it is like a water that doesn't quench my thirst. I need more.

Our quest may take time, and I feel you will not forgive me if we don't return for a brief visit before it begins. You will meet Spindrift, and when I show you all the orchids I am keeping with me, you will understand why I could not stop.

I do fear that someone will try to take them from me, and to protect Spindrift I mustn't make the Masdevallia *too tempting a target. I have hidden the blue one for now, safe in the knowledge that its power is mine.*

Love,

Emilie

"Orchid," said Spindrift with surprising calmness, her fingers closing around the glass. Max stood and placed another ribboned pin in the map.

"Yes, Spindrift?"

"I wish for you to take the ship here," she said, pointing at the coordinates. "As fast as you can." Immediately the *Masdevallia* tilted to one side as it turned sharply in the water, paper, quills, pins, lamps sliding from the table onto the floor. The three of them grabbed whatever solid thing was nearest and held on until the ship righted itself again, Max's face turning slightly green. Thinking more clearly than the others, Clémence righted the lamps before their flames could cause disaster.

Spindrift searched among the mess, looking for the letter's pair. Finally, she found it and sat where she was on the floor to read.

18th day of the Month of Endings, in the Year of the Stars
N 48°51'24", E 2°21'03"

My dearest Emilie,
To say I am proud is an understatement of the highest order. It is not just your success at finding the orchids that pleases me, but also that you are so clearly more able to resist them than I was. The very fact that you parted with one, if only to hide it, shows that you don't share my weaknesses. Well done.
Love,
Papa

A warm glow suffused Spindrift through her slight confusion. This was the second time that Grandfather's letters had hinted at his own search for the orchids and his failure to find them. If that were true, it was the only time Spindrift knew of that he hadn't found some magical object he wanted.

It was almost dawn when Clémence insisted they get another few hours of sleep so that they were rested for whatever came next. Spindrift didn't feel tired, but the motion of the ship was soothing, and the hammock folded around her like one of Grandfather's hugs. Her eyelids grew heavy, and eventually fell closed.

Bright sun streamed through the portholes; Spindrift blinked herself awake. Her mouth was dry, lips cracked and caked with salt. Quickly, she sat up, and just as quickly she was on the floor, pain rattling her bones.

"Spin! Are you okay?" Clémence asked, awoken by the crash, peering over the edge of her hammock.

"Y-yes," said Spindrift, rubbing her arm, "but I suggest you climb out carefully."

Nothing seemed broken, only sore enough to remind Spindrift of her own silliness. Safely on her feet, she found Orchid so she could wish for fresh water.

Ah. That was better. Max and Clémence gratefully finished off the flagons before following Spindrift up onto the deck.

There was no land anywhere, just sunlight and blue. They stood at the bow, wind ripping through their hair and the spaces between their grinning teeth.

Whatever danger lay ahead, in this moment Spindrift was as happy as she could remember being. She understood what her mother had meant now when she'd said being on the water felt like her destiny. Something enormous and finned crested a wave and disappeared again into the depths.

Fathomless depths. Spindrift wasn't frightened, but it was nicer to not think about that. Clémence asked if she could fetch the telescope from below, and they took turns looking through it, searching the surface for more creatures. Max had it now, his head turning this way and that. Suddenly he jerked the lens back to where it had been an instant before. "Spin?" he said.

It took her a moment to resight the telescope, following his pointing finger until she found what he'd seen. Another ship in the distance, which seemed to be moving as quickly as they were, which is to say it looked as though it wasn't moving at all. Of course, it could be any ship, hundreds at least must sail these seas, moving silks and spices and even real orchids whose scents would fill the holds with perfume.

She twitched the telescope upward.

Not just any ship would have a flag that was eerily similar to the one that flew high above her head. A red orchid on a black background to the *Masdevallia*'s black orchid on a white background.

"It's him," she said. The crystal ball was heavy in her pocket. "Orchid?"

"Yes, Spindrift?"

"Follow that ship."

She paced up and down the deck, willing the *Masdevallia* to catch up to Roland. The sun arced through the sky and started to fall, setting both clouds and ocean alight. The sails whipped and snapped above her. Clémence and Max had gone down to the galley to eat the food Spindrift had wished for them, but she wasn't hungry. They needed to get to the port before Roland. The last orchid needed to be hers! It had belonged to her mother; it was rightfully Spindrift's now!

"You're talking to yourself," said Max. She wheeled around, and he stepped backward, fright etched on his face.

"What?" asked Spindrift, feeling normal again. She hadn't quite been herself for a second there.

"Nothing." Max shook his head. "Are you all right?"

She wished people would stop asking her that. She was perfectly fine. She simply needed to stop Roland. If she didn't, she and Grandfather would never be safe. She'd be forced to surrender the black orchid or otherwise get rid of it somehow just so that Roland would leave them alone.

"Yes," she said. "Yes, I'm all right."

"I thought you might be cold," he said, and now in the gathering darkness she could see a blanket in his hands. "You've been out here almost all day."

"Thank you," she said. It occurred to her that this could possibly be the longest conversation she'd ever had with Max alone. The thought broke her distraction with the ship in the distance, and she realized her teeth were chattering. "I-I t-think I-I'll c-come inside, t-though."

"Oh, good."

She wished up tea, which wasn't as good as Grandfather's but was nonetheless blissfully hot and sweet with sugar. The three of them sat around the table in the galley, emptying their cups before they opened the box of letters again. There was nothing else to do; the ship took care of itself, and all they could do was wait until they caught up to Roland or reached the port to discover they were too late.

25th day of the Month of Endings, in the Year of the Stars
N 0°20', E 6°44'

Dearest Papa,

I'm not entirely certain why I am continuing to write when we will be in Lux before any of these letters arrive there, but it seems to be a habit I cannot break. Besides, it is a good distraction, a good reminder that I am coming home to visit when all I truly wish to do is continue my search for the remaining orchids. Those members of the crew who don't know what our true purpose is—and they are idiots not to have figured it out, quite honestly—are thrilled with the promise of reuniting with their families, however briefly. We will not be staying long. Only a few of the orchids are mine thus far and it is not enough.

Not enough.

Not enough! I must have them all!

Love,

Emilie

The handwriting looked as if someone had dipped a spider in ink and set it free to run as it would across the paper. Spindrift read it four times before she was sure she understood all of it.

"Is it just me," said Clémence, "or does she sound as if she was starting to go a bit mad?"

Anger tore through Spindrift like an explosion. "She wasn't mad!" she yelled, jumping up from the table and knocking several letters to the floor. "She knew what the orchids meant, that's all! They are important! Gifts from the Sages themselves! Don't talk like that about my mother!"

"Calm down!" yelled Clémence. "Do you think I didn't see how you looked at me when I touched your precious orchid? They're just wishes, Spin!"

Spindrift ran from the galley, through the nearest door, slamming it behind her. Her parents' bed was soft and cool, and she buried her face into the pillows.

This time, unlike when she'd run to her bedroom at home, they didn't leave her alone. She wanted to be left alone. But the door opened and the corner of the bed dipped down as someone sat on it.

"I think you need to remember what your Grandfather said in *his* letter about your mother," said Clémence quietly. "Max said you frightened him earlier. These orchids do something to people, Spin."

Spindrift said nothing. The pillow was wet from her angry breath, but she didn't move her head.

"He said something else, too, before. Your grandfather, I mean. Remember when he was telling us the story? *More curse than wish*, he said. I think he was right."

Spindrift stayed silent. The moment drew out between

them like a note from a violin string on the nights Grandfather had taken her to the symphony.

"Fine," said Clémence. "Think about this, then. Be nice, or we'll make you wish us back home and you'll be all alone out here."

If she'd been in the hammock, she would have fallen out again, Spindrift sat up so quickly. "No!" she said. "No. I'm sorry." She didn't know how to explain what was happening inside her, the way the pull of the orchids came and went.

"If you were really sorry, you'd wish us up an apple tart," said Clémence. "And some hot water for a bath. I found a metal tub large enough."

Spindrift did both, and cream for the tart as well. Cleaned and fed, they sat again around the table in a slightly uneasy peace. She reached for the next envelope, steeling herself against what might be within. Clémence was right; the orchids did things to people. The only thing worse than what they'd done to her mother was what might happen if Roland collected all of them. Spindrift had to be careful. She must remember that she didn't want all the orchids for herself.

Did she?

No, she told herself firmly, recalling Clémence's words, Grandfather's warning.

*29th day of the Month of Endings, in the Year of
the Stars
N 48°51'24", E 2°21'03"*

*My dearest Emilie,
Now I am worried. Please come home. We must talk.
  Love,
  Papa*

*3rd day of the Month of Origins, in the Year of the
Ephemeral
N 6°18'48", W 10°48'5"*

*Dearest Papa,
We have stopped off in port to trade some ordinary cargo. This is all such a waste of time. The
most avid horticulturalist wouldn't understand
my need to collect my orchids. They are out there,
waiting for me. Theo is as impatient as I am—he
nearly threw Philippe off the ship yesterday for
suggesting we stay closer to home after visiting
Lux. Even Theo doesn't understand, though, not
truly.
    The orchids are mine, not his. They will never
be his.*

Love,

Emilie

9th day of the Month of Origins, in the Year of the Ephemeral
N 48°51'24", E 2°21'03"

My dearest Emilie,
I see it taking you now as it took me. You MUST RESIST. To reunite the orchids is a noble goal, but not at the expense of your mind. Think of Theo and little Spindrift. If you will not come home, be strong.

Love,

Papa

11th day of the Month of Origins, in the Year of the Ephemeral
N 6°45'0", W 11°22'0"

Dearest Papa,
I'm beginning to suspect a traitor in our midst. Roland, who is in on the secret, is asking far too many questions about the orchids, particularly about where in port I hid the blue one. He claims

that if we are set upon by pirates again and some-
thing happens to myself and Theo, someone should
remain who knows. I have put him off for now,
while keeping in mind something might need to be
done about this problem.

    My blades are sharp, as ever.

    Love,

    Emilie

Three months later, the *Masdevallia* sank, but it had been Roland who sank it. Her mother hadn't—as she put it—taken care of the problem. Spindrift stared at the crystal ball in its nest of cotton and wondered how Roland had managed it when her mother had the power of the orchids to call upon. Couldn't she have wished for the *Masdevallia* to be safe? For her and Spindrift's father to live?

Though they already knew where they were going, Max continued to put pins in the map on the wall. Perhaps it simply gave him something to do. Clémence read each letter as Spindrift finished with it, though surely she did not get the same sick feeling as was in the pit of Spindrift's stomach.

21st day of the Month of Origins, in the Year of the
Ephemeral
N 28°28', W 16°15'

Dearest Papa,

These letters are the only thing that make sense anymore, because I know you understand about the orchids. You taught me to see the magic in objects, the promise of wonder. I caught Spindrift reaching for my black orchid yesterday and I nearly struck her. I would have if Theo had not caught me in time. I must do better at keeping their importance to myself, though Theo did not blame me. He understood. The light in his eyes is like a fever, and if I looked in the mirror I'm sure I would see the same.

Roland seems unusually content with himself. Perhaps he enjoyed the pleasures of this port more than I predicted. It was I who insisted upon stopping here; it felt like the right place to refill our stores. Spindrift must be kept fed and clothed so that one day she may understand this quest. I hope by the time she is old enough to know about it at all we will have completed it. She will know her mother as the Eighth Sage, the one who succeeded in reuniting the seven where everyone else has failed. Even you.

Love,

Emilie

30th day of the Month of Endings, in the Year of
the Ephemeral
N 48°51'24", E 2°21'03"

My dearest Emilie,
If you will not come to the truth, it will come to
you, and here it is.

The black orchid revealed itself to me when I
was older than you are now. I found it among my
mother's things when she passed; she had never told
me of its secrets, and to my knowledge she never
made a single wish. Perhaps that is the type of per-
son who should possess them, but it is too late for
that now.

Your mother and I were married by then, and
I shared the blooming of the black orchid with her
as soon as it happened. I read all that I could, spoke
to others, learned of its origins and its connection to
our bloodline. I knew I must unite them.

You were already born, and so your mother
stayed in Lux with you, while I set sail that very
month. I didn't see you take your first toddling step,
or hear you speak your first words.

They drove me mad, my dearest, as they are
doing to you, but the worst was yet to come. I was

foolish, you see, to think my quest had gone unno-
ticed by others, and I was foolish to think that their
attentions would be focused on me.

Someone was certain I had kept an orchid in
our beautiful home. Your mother fought them off
as best she could, but . . .

At least you survived. I abandoned my ship, my
quest as soon as word came and flew home on a pair
of wings, bringing only the black orchid with me. I
should have thrown it into the ocean, but I couldn't
bear to. Nonetheless, I never made a single wish
with it again, and never will. I gave it to you not
only because it is rightfully yours, but also because
I cannot bear to touch it, knowing its cost.

Learn from my mistakes, chérie. *I beg you.*
Love,
Papa

Spindrift dropped the letter on the table. And the night
exploded with the unmistakable sound of cannon fire.

CHAPTER FOURTEEN

So Near, So Far

IN THE DEAD OF NIGHT, the cannonballs exploding from the nearby ship cast light on the water like fireworks. One whizzed past the bow of the *Masdevallia* so close by that Spindrift, on the deck now, heard it whistle.

Just beyond Roland's vessel, the light of the port touched the darkness. They had caught up, but it was clear he had no intention of letting them join him on land.

"How can he see us?" Clémence shouted. "I thought you protected the ship! You wished for it!"

I have wishes too, little girl. More of them than you do.

"Orchid!" screamed Spindrift, the glass cold in her hand.

"Hello, Spindrift." In the pitch blackness all Spindrift could see of Orchid were her pale face, long-fingered hands, lips as red as blood.

"I wish you to fire the cannons!"

The *Masdevallia* shook ferociously, cannonballs loosed and, seconds later, splashed into the water.

Oh. She was her parents' daughter, but not a sailor yet. The cannons shot from the side of the ship, not the front.

"I wish for you to turn us to the left!" she yelled.

Spindrift, Max, and Clémence slid across the deck, crashing painfully into the railings as the *Masdevallia* spun in place. "I wish for you to fire the cannons again!" she said, scrabbling for purchase on the wet, freezing deck.

The cannonballs missed again, but not by nearly so much. "I wish for you to hit that ship!"

The water carried the sound of splintering wood to their ears.

"Maybe it'll sink now!" said Clémence, but Spindrift, on her feet, knew better. She couldn't see Orchid in the darkness, but Roland had ones that weren't black. Above the deck of the other ship, colors glowed like the filament lamps on the streets of Lux. Red, orange, yellow, green, purple.

"He's fixing it," she whispered to herself. "Orchid, I wish for you to protect us!"

Just in time. An enormous ball of steel hit the *Masdevallia*'s bow with a thundering *crack*, but the ship did not break. "I wish for you to hit that ship again!" she cried.

Over and over, the two ships traded blows. Spindrift wished for more cannonballs, picturing the used ones littering the ocean floor. She wished for gunpowder and warmth and tea to soothe her burning throat. They were trapped, not receiving any damage but not causing any, either.

"Maybe someone will come and help us?" suggested Clémence.

Max shook his head. "Why would they risk themselves? It's not their business. Better no one comes to help than they choose to help him instead."

Spindrift's ears rang, and her head ached. She wished she had a sword to press to Roland's chest as Grandfather had done.

The useless sword dropped from her hand, hitting the deck with a clatter.

Dawn blushed pink across the sky, casting light on the silvery fins breaking free of the waves around them. Spindrift counted one minute, two, three without another attempt from Roland. Just beyond him was a harbor where ships even grander than the *Masdevallia* rose to the sky.

"Do you think he's really given up?" Spindrift asked.

"I think he thought he could get us while we were sleeping," said Max.

"But how did he know it was us?" asked Clémence, and Max pointed to the flag above. "We were in the galley. We must have neared enough for him to see us. He used to quartermaster this ship. He knows the *Masdevallia*."

She was grateful for them both, but Spindrift wondered if she would have made it even this far without Max. By the breaking daylight, they saw the other ship trim its sails and move toward the harbor. The *Masdevallia* was still farther away; Roland would get a head start. "Orchid," she began. "I wish for you to take us—"

"No," interrupted Max. "Spin, he sabotaged this ship once before." He pointed a little way up from the port, which was in a secluded bay. "Hide the ship around the hill and we'll take one of those smaller boats to land."

She didn't have a better idea. "Orchid, I wish for you to do as Max says."

Soon they were climbing into a tiny boat, knocking their knees against the paddles rigged to the sides. Spindrift looked around, overcome by a memory of a memory. She had been in one of these before. Max took up the oars, his face soon glistening with sweat, hair crackling in the rising heat.

"Faster, Max!" Clémence snapped. "He's going to find it before we even get there!"

Spindrift opened her mouth but said nothing. Max had been such a help, but Clémence might be right. And if Roland found the blue orchid, there would be nothing to stop him from coming after the three of them again. Alone on the water, and with Roland possessed of the same obsession she had seen in her mother's letters, her orchid might not be enough to protect them.

"Orchid, I wish for the boat to go faster," she said, but she whispered it so Max wouldn't hear it over the splashing of the water.

The boat sped up, the oars moving at a blur, and Max's arms with them. He looked up and grinned at Spindrift, knowing what she'd done.

The bay was purest blue. Rainbow-colored fish darted about the boat, their fins catching the brilliant sunlight. Spindrift and Clémence fanned themselves with their hands and Max's slipped on the wood as he tried to steer them alongside a weather-beaten jetty. People in bright clothes pointed at them and shouted to each other in a language Spindrift didn't understand.

One of them, who looked a bit like he could be Max's older brother, gave Spindrift a white-toothed smile and threw down a fraying rope. She didn't know as many knots as Emilie, but she tied the boat as best she could, hoping it wouldn't float away while they were gone.

It was a relief to be on land. Spindrift's legs wobbled beneath her, unused to solid ground. Clémence swayed gently back and forth.

The man who'd thrown her the rope said something, a smile still on his face, and Spindrift shook her head. She reached into her pocket, the glass of the orb the coolest thing in the baking day.

"Orchid?" Spindrift whispered.

"Yes, Spindrift?" replied the orchid, just as quietly.

"I wish to be able to speak to them and understand them."

"I cannot do that to you," said the orchid, and a sort of frustrated disappointment welled within Spindrift until Orchid spoke again. "Perhaps, yes, it is worth a try. Please, give me a moment."

Spindrift sensed Orchid's concentration, the ball getting hotter and hotter in her pocket. She yelped and yanked her hand back in time to see tiny blisters form on her fingertips . . . and for a small, smooth, gray pebble to appear in her palm.

"We are lucky," said Orchid, "there was one nearby. A language stone. You may have come across them in your grandfather's shop on occasion."

Spindrift had, once. Grandfather had shown her how to use it. She closed her hand around the pebble and squeezed.

"Where did you come from?" asked the man. He looked at Max, who shook his head. Spindrift shook hers. She'd heard his words in her ear, and another set, one she could comprehend, inside her head. "Little children in a boat!"

"Our parents are on our ship," said Spindrift, waving her hand vaguely in the direction of the *Masdevallia*. "We came to look for—" It was difficult to think quickly in the heat. "Our uncle! We came to look for our uncle. Our ships were supposed to meet here. Tall man? Dark suit?"

"Ahhhh," said Spindrift's new friend, nodding. "Yes, I think I saw him. He went into the markets." He pointed over his shoulder at a mass of huts that sloped gently up and away from the harbor.

"Thank you," said Spindrift. The man nodded, his eyes following the odd little group as they moved into the bustling port. Here and there Spindrift caught a word she recognized; clearly ships from many places stopped here, and it struck her that she might be standing in the same place her parents once had.

They felt so close and so far away, all at the same time.

• • •

It was cooler in the market, the stalls and shops covered with cloths that kept out the worst of the heat. For an hour they pushed through the crowds, their noses wrinkling at the scents of fish and spices. Every time Spindrift thought she glimpsed Roland, it turned out to be a shadow or a sailor in a uniform that reminded Spindrift of her black wool dress. The lanes between the stalls were crooked, tangled; more than once they turned a corner only to find they'd already seen that display of carved wood or silks.

A young woman sold water filled with lemon slices. It wasn't the lemonade from the corners of Magothire Street, but it was cool and welcome, Spindrift's wished-for coins buying as much as she, Clémence, and Max could drink.

"Where *is* he?" Clémence said when her throat was no longer so dry she couldn't speak.

Spindrift shrugged and took a deep breath. She was trying to stay calm, but if they didn't find him soon, he was going to find the blue orchid without them.

And the blue orchid is mine. They are all mine.

"Spin?" asked Max.

"I'm fine," she said. "Just hot." She felt in her pocket for the cold glass. The orchids called to each other. Her mother had said so, and Spindrift's orchid herself had said that once she'd felt something, as if she wasn't alone.

"Orchid?"

"Yes, Spindrift?"

"Do you . . . feel anything?"

"I feel many things, Spindrift," said Orchid almost sadly.

"I mean right now. Do you feel anything unusual?"

People flowed around them, bright as flowers, chattering in fifty different tongues, but Spindrift was only listening for Orchid's answer.

"No," said Orchid finally. "I don't think so. Am I supposed to feel something?"

Spindrift didn't answer. She looked up and down the stalls; a flash of brass in sunlight caught her eye. Making sure Clémence and Max were right behind her so she didn't lose them in the crowd, she pushed forward.

The stall, a sort of three-sided hut, was dark and smelled of something spicy-sweet. A set of wind chimes hung from a corner, the brass that had attracted Spindrift. A breeze was blowing, but they were silent.

She combed her mind for music, any music. A tune began to play in her head, a melody from the last time Grandfather had taken her to the opera.

The chimes joined in, echoing her thoughts the way the translated speech did. Clairvoyant.

She went inside.

The man in the shadows didn't *look* like Grand-father, but there was something about him, a sort of Grandfatherishness that Spindrift recognized.

"Hello," she said.

"Hello," said the man, nodding. His eyes flicked from Spindrift to Clémence and Max. "What do you seek, children?" He had a cloth pressed to his forehead, likely mopping up sweat caused by the heat of the day.

Clémence turned away to inspect a basket full of silken butterflies. Whatever magic they held would involve flying; perhaps they took messages in the same way as Grandfather's clockwork birds. Perhaps they were a plaything that hatched from caterpillars and turned back again.

"I'm looking for something specific," said Spindrift.

"Oh, yes?" The man smiled.

"Well, it's . . . it's difficult to explain."

"Go on," he said.

"It's a flower," said Spindrift. "A blue flower, one that blooms as you look at it."

The man's eyes widened. Slowly he walked toward Spindrift, his hands raised in a placating gesture, the cloth dropping away from his forehead. Now Spindrift saw the cut, the blood. "I have never seen it!" he said. "I promise you, I don't know where it is!"

Excitement, horror, fear roiled together in Spindrift's

chest. "But you've heard of it?" she asked. "You know what I'm talking about."

"I know of it. I do not have it!" His voice shook with terror.

"I know," said Spindrift, kindly as she could. "I believe you. I think it is hidden here, somewhere in this port. Where would somebody hide such a thing?"

The man's whole body was trembling now. "I already told the other one, check the caves!"

"Where?"

He pointed.

"Thank you," said Spindrift, whirling around and grabbing Clémence and Max. She pulled them through the crowds, her eyes peeled for anything that looked like the mouth of a cave. She hoped caves looked the same way they were described in books. Then she might have a hope of finding it.

They broke free of the market, into a street so like Nightbrick Lane, Spindrift wondered for an instant whether she'd accidentally wished herself home, before she remembered Orchid couldn't do that. And there were differences; lines of washing crisscrossed overhead, drying in the sun, and this one didn't wind its way up a hill; it simply wandered along and ended abruptly at a sheer wall of rock.

A narrow path clung to the side of the cliff. Spindrift

did the one thing she probably shouldn't have done; she looked down. It wasn't a terribly long drop to the shallow waters, but she had absolutely no desire to see how long it would take before she made a splash. In a single line, she, Clémence, and Max edged their way forward.

There was a crack in the cliff face about twenty yards along, just wide enough for a fully grown person to squeeze through. It was easier for Spindrift, who stepped easily into a large chamber of water-smoothed rock. It was dark but blessedly cool, the air musty and tinged with salt. A hand grasped at her, and she jumped.

"It's me," said Clémence. Her voice echoed.

"Oh." Spindrift felt blindly for the crystal ball and wished for a light. The cave filled with a blue glow like that of the alchemist's dish beside her bed.

Was Grandfather all right without her?

She could see the tunnel now, leading deeper into the cliff.

"I don't like this," said Max.

"Do you want to stay here?" his sister asked without a trace of mocking.

Max shook his head. All together and slowly, they began to make their way forward. Something—many somethings—rustled overhead. Water dripped in precise time with Spindrift's quickened heartbeat.

The caves were really a series of small rooms joined together by a path, each chamber larger than the last. Max's breathing came a little easier in each one, the rock walls not pressing in quite so heavily upon him. It didn't bother Spindrift so much, but she understood. She wouldn't choose to live in here.

"Orchid?" she asked.

"Yes, Spindrift?"

"Remember when you told me you once felt like you weren't alone? I need you to tell me if you feel like that again. I wish for you to tell me."

"I will," said Orchid.

Spindrift knew they were likely already too late; Roland had probably come and gone. He knew this port, if not the cave itself. He hadn't been with Emilie when she'd hidden the blue orchid here, but he would have found this place faster than Spindrift, Max, and Clémence had today.

Still, she had to look. Her mother had come through here. She had to see it, even if that meant seeing the empty space where the blue orchid had been until an hour ago.

Clémence yanked on the back of Spindrift's shirt, nearly choking her. "Stop!" Clémence whispered. "I hear something!"

Spindrift heard things too, dripping water and leathery wings. She didn't think that's what Clémence meant. She strained her ears and shook her head.

"I don't hear anything."

"I . . ." Clémence paused. "I was *sure* I did."

The next room rose above them like the ceiling of a cathedral. The blue glow flickered, gathering strength until it reached the very edges of the cave.

"Spindrift?" said her orchid. "I feel something!"

On the other side of the cave stood Roland, a set of empty crystal balls hovering in a circle around his shoulders, his orchids waiting for his wishes.

Spindrift froze, and the weight of her own foolishness crushed the air from her chest. She'd thought they could stop Roland, or that he would fetch the blue orchid and leave here. But why would he have done that? He knew they were following, and the black orchid was the last he needed.

Her feet refused her order to run.

"Hello, Spindrift," said Roland in his smooth, quiet voice. It was difficult to imagine that voice giving orders aboard a ship.

Max tugged on Spindrift's arm and whispered in her ear. Spindrift squinted through the gloom, counting.

The blue orchid wasn't here. Only five spun slowly around him. Disappointment and relief warred within her.

"Where is it?" he said, taking a step toward them. "Tell me where it is and I will let you live."

"I don't know!" said Spindrift, forcing the words from her dry throat.

"I think you do. She may not have told me, but Emilie would have told someone. You survived. Are you telling me her hiding place did not survive with you?" He was even closer now.

"I don't know where it is. I promise!"

Clémence screamed—a choked, muffled scream. Roland had moved with lighting speed to put his arm around her throat. Clémence's dark eyes met Spindrift's, begging, pleading. Beside Spindrift, Max was paralyzed with terror.

"She told me with her dying breath that this is where it was. I doubt you are so skilled a liar as your mother, Spindrift. Would you like to tell me where it is with your little friend's dying breath?"

His eyes shone as he stared at her. The five orbs still floated around Roland, and now Clémence, too. He was distracted.

She could grab one.

Clémence would understand.

Maybe even two.

Clémence wheezed, her eyes bulging as Roland

squeezed the life from her. Max's mouth opened in a soundless scream.

If she had three, and Roland had three . . . She met Clémence's eyes again, and the spell broke, fear spilling hotly through her.

"Stop!" Spindrift yelled, the word repeating over and over as it echoed around the enormous cave. "Take it!" She held out the black orchid, the crystal ball gleaming in her palm. "Take it! Just let her go!"

Coughing and spluttering, Clémence fell to the ground. Max ran to her.

Roland's fingers brushed the top of the black orchid. His strange smile returned.

"No," he said, pulling his hand away. "Not yet."

CHAPTER FIFTEEN

Two

SILENCE RANG THROUGH THE GALLEY of the *Masdevallia*. They'd spoken little on the journey back, each consumed by their own thoughts. The feast Spindrift had wished for still covered the table, nearly untouched. In the middle of it all sat the black orchid on a nest of wadded cotton.

Why hadn't he taken it from her?

"Let's go over this again," said Spindrift to break the smothering quiet. "We haven't finished reading the letters. Maybe they say something else."

Without a word, Clémence stood and disappeared into the room where Spindrift's parents had slept, closing the door behind her.

"She saw the way you looked at the orchids," said Max.

Spindrift's stomach turned over. That meant he had, too. Did they both hate her now?

"I think you can't help yourself, so I don't hate you," he said, answering the question as if she had spoken aloud. "We already know they do things to people. Do you remember why we're doing this?"

"So that Roland doesn't get all seven and harness the full power of the Sages."

"Do you want it instead?"

"No."

"Hold on to that," said Max. "Whatever happens, hold on to that. That's what your Grandfather's letters warned your mother about, and she couldn't stop it. You have to, Spindrift."

Spindrift nodded. She would try as hard as she could. The contents of Grandfather's last letter were still too much to think about. "I just don't understand why he didn't take it from me."

Max pushed away his plate, stood, and walked to the map on the wall. "I think I might," he said.

"Why?"

"Would you be able to sail the *Masdevallia* without your orchid?"

No, of course not. Spindrift shook her head. She

had the blood of sailors, true, but she hadn't grown up on this or any ship. She didn't know how to trim a sail or tie more than the most basic of knots. She didn't know what to do in a storm or how to safely steer the ship into a harbor. Even if she did, the *Masdevallia* was a large ship. Without the magic of the wishes, it would need a large crew. She still didn't see what Max was trying to say.

"He's waiting to see what we do next," said Max.

"But we followed him here," Spindrift protested. "He knows I don't know where it is."

"Yy-es," said Max, nodding slowly, "but the last person who *did* know was your mother. He'll wait to see if you think of anything. I'm sure of it."

"And if I do—which I won't because I have no idea—but if I do, I need the black orchid to help me sail."

"Exactly. Which is why he won't hurt us now," said Max, more sure of himself than Spindrift thought was strictly fair given the day's events. She closed her eyes and remembered the light in Roland's. *Like a fever*, her mother had said of her father.

"But he's right behind us," said Spindrift. His ship was close enough that she could read the name *Cymbidium* painted across its hull.

"He'll wait," said Max.

Well, he could wait. It was somewhat satisfying to imagine him on the deck of the *Cymbidium* getting angrier and angrier as the *Masdevallia* bobbed on the surface of the water, its anchor heavy on the ocean floor. Not as satisfying as it would be to know where the blue orchid was, however. And definitely not as satisfying as it would be if Clémence forgave her.

It was Spindrift's turn to open the cabin door and see her friend lying on the bed. A livid bruise spread across Clémence's neck, and her eyes were wet.

"I'm sorry, Clém," whispered Spindrift. "I didn't mean to."

It was Clémence's turn to not answer. Spindrift knelt on the edge of the bed, trying to get Clémence to look at her, but Clémence's pretty dark eyes remained steadfastly fixed on the ceiling. "It's the orchids."

"Of course," said Clémence hoarsely. "The orchids. I think you should be pleased, Spin. All your life you've wanted to be just like your mother, and now you are."

The words hit Spindrift like a blow. She *didn't* want to be like her mother. The traces of Emilie in the letters toward the end of the box were horrible.

"It won't happen again," she promised.

Clémence sat up, and relief flooded through Spindrift. She needed her friend back if they were going to figure out what to do next. Clémence was clever and brave and wonderful.

"You're right," said Clémence. "Because I'm going home."

Spindrift's blood ran cold. "What?"

"You heard me. I want to go home. I want off this awful ship, and I don't care about the orchids." Spindrift could tell the last bit was a lie, but did it really matter?

"You can't!"

"Oh, can't I? Are you telling me what to do now?" Clémence scrambled off the bed and strode into the galley. Spindrift could only watch as she swiped the orchid from the table and ran upstairs to the deck. By the time Spindrift and Max caught up with her, Clémence was leaning over the railing, the crystal ball held above the restless water.

"Say you'll wish me home!" Clémence shouted into the wind. "Say it, or say good-bye to your precious orchid!"

Spindrift shot a panicked look at Max, who seemed nearly as frightened. Rain began to fall, from a few drops to a torrent in an instant. Spindrift's eyes filled with water that may have been tears. "I can't!" she screamed. "I can't wish things about people! I would if I could!" She blinked her eyes clear in time to see Clémence pulling her arm back, the orchid safe again.

"Then I'll take the wings," said Clémence coldly.

Spindrift's heart ached as if it had been run through with a sword. "And what about you?" Clémence asked, staring at Max.

Max licked his lips, casting his eyes between the two of them. "I can't leave her alone, Clém. Go home to Maman and Papa. Tell them we're all right."

Rage snapped in Clémence's eyes like lightning to go with the storm. The crystal ball was slippery, slick as she passed it to Spindrift, waiting.

The orchid bloomed, floating above the deck, her dress of air and midnight unaffected by the rain. Spindrift wasn't sure how she could feel like she was drowning and yet have a throat so dry she could barely speak, both at the same time.

"Orchid," she said.

"Yes, Spindrift?"

"I wish to summon the red wings from below."

Instantly they were on the deck, bright as a smear of blood between Spindrift and Clémence. Tears streamed down Spindrift's face, and she coughed big, choking sobs. More than anything she wanted to beg Clémence to stay. Clémence was her family of a kind, and so were the orchids, and so was Grandfather, and Spindrift felt as if she would fly apart from being pulled in so many directions.

And so she said nothing. She turned away so she wouldn't have to watch Max help Clémence fasten the wings to her back or see Clémence's feet leave the deck.

"Wait!" she shouted, whirling around. Clémence hovered in the air, too much like the orchid for comfort. Rather than wish it, as she'd done with the wings, Spindrift again begged Clémence to wait and ran down the stairs to the galley to search frantically for the compass.

"Here," she said when she returned with it, standing on her toes and reaching as high as she could. Clémence's fingers brushed hers as they closed around the compass that would show Clémence the direction in which Lux lay, the place she most wanted to go.

Something warm splashed onto Spindrift's forehead, much warmer than the rain. Clémence wiped her eyes with the back of her empty hand and nodded.

And then, standing on the rain-lashed deck, soaked to their skins, there were two.

The *Masdevallia* seemed quieter than it should after the loss of only one of them. Perhaps it was that Clémence didn't just have part of Max's voice, but some of Spindrift's as well. Perhaps it was simply that she and Max sat in the galley, unable to bring themselves to speak.

It was all her fault. She didn't deserve Max staying, and yet she would wish Clémence back in a heartbeat if such a wish would work. Trivial wishes, like clearing away the forgotten feast, seemed so useless now.

More curse than wish, Grandfather had said. She hoped one day Clémence would forgive her.

With nothing else to do, Spindrift got out the box of letters. They were jumbled now, out of order and some were probably in the wrong envelopes, but Grandfather's slip of red card marked the place she'd last reached. Once again, her mother's handwriting was messier than in the previous letter. Spindrift could finally see this for the slow descent into madness that it was.

> *27th day of the Month of Origins, in the Year of the*
> *Ephemeral*
> *N 28°29'46.47", W 11°19'57.65"*
>
> *Dearest Papa,*
> *We will be further delayed. There is another one*
> *nearby. I know it. They sing to me like wind*
> *chimes. My power grows stronger every day.*
> *I know you'll understand.*
> *Love,*
> *Emilie*

1st day of the Month of Glass, in the Year of the
Ephemeral
N 31°30'47", W 9°46'11"

Dearest Papa,
It is here. I know it is! Why can I not find it! Why
does it resist me so? IT WILL BE MINE!
  Love,
  Emilie

13th day of the Month of Glass, in the Year of the
Ephemeral
N 33°32'0", W 7°35'0"

Dearest Papa,
Most of our crew have deserted us. They say they do
not want to sail a ship captained by madmen. Fools!
We do not need them. We do not need anyone! We
still have enough men to keep going, all of whom
know our secret, and we still have Spindrift. That
is all that matters. Even Roland left us, to which I
say good riddance. I do not trust him.
  If there was an orchid here, it is gone. There is
a beautiful arch in the harbor here that reminds me
of the ones in Lux. We are coming home.

Love,

Emilie

29th day of the Month of Glass, in the Year of the
Ephemeral
N 42°52'57", W 9°16'20"

Dearest Papa,
We have stopped for food and supplies. I am not
hungry, I want only my orchids.
    Love,
    Emilie

1st Day of the Month of Rains, in the Year of the
Ephemeral
N 48°51'24", E 2°21'03"

My dearest Emilie,
If you will not stop, I am coming to stop you. For
your own sake, and for Spindrift's, and for mine. I
can watch the orchids take you from me no longer.
    Love,
    Papa

Wait.

"He came to the *Masdevallia*?" Spindrift said aloud. Max left his usual spot by the map to come over and read the note. "But he wasn't on it when it sank."

"Maybe he didn't have a chance to get to it," said Max. "He might not even have had a chance to leave Lux."

Spindrift's eyes burned; she could read no more tonight. Paper crinkled under Max's touch as he pressed a pin into the place matching the last letter's coordinates, and Spindrift rested her pounding head in her hands.

The woman who wrote those letters had ceased to be her mother, had ceased to be Emilie. She was something else.

"Let's go to bed, Spin," said Max softly. "We'll keep looking in the morning."

Spindrift nodded, but she ignored the siren call of the hammock and climbed the narrow stairs to the deck instead. The *Cymbidium* was still there, not far away, watching, waiting to see what she'd do next. Rain streamed off its sails.

She wished—

No. She didn't wish she was back home in Lux, safe with Grandfather, but she did want this all to be over.

The absence of Clémence's breathing beside her when Spindrift finally climbed into bed was loud in the night. She tossed and turned, jolting awake every time she nearly fell out of the hammock. Her eyes were fully open by the time the sky turned pink outside the portholes, and even then she looked over, expecting to see Clémence a foot away.

The rain had stopped sometime while they slept, or at least while Max had slept, though Spindrift wasn't sure he was any more rested than she was. She wished up some hot water, and Max went to wash in the tub Clémence had found while Spindrift made all the delicious breakfast foods she could think of appear on the table.

Neither one of them was particularly hungry, even after their scant meal the night before. They picked at eggs and kippers, croissants and fruits slathered with cream.

"Maybe we should just go home," said Spindrift. The light of day, rather than improving the situation, seemed only to illuminate the hopelessness growing inside her. She had lost Clémence, and she didn't know where the blue orchid was, and the answer couldn't be in any of the remaining letters. If Emilie had written to say where she'd hidden it, Grandfather would have known. He would have told Spindrift to look for *that* one, not the one containing the false clue.

"No, Spin. Not yet," said Max. "We can do this. I know we can. Besides, if we go home, Roland will keep looking, and once he finds the blue one, he'll come after you. I don't want anything to happen to you."

She scrambled across the bench and buried her face in

his shoulder. Max patted her back, waiting for her tears to stop soaking the collar of his shirt.

"Come on," he said. "Let's get back to reading."

First, she needed some fresh air. Telescope in hand, she went up to the deck, scanning the *Cymbidium* for any signs of life. It was too much to hope that Roland had abandoned it.

He stood by the *Cymbidium*'s bowsprit, waving at her. Disgusted, she returned to the galley and took a handful of envelopes from the wooden box. On all but one of them the addresses were barely legible, and the papers inside them were worse. Nonsensical scribbles, huge splotches of black ink, tears where Emilie had stabbed the quill too fiercely. Frantic, Spindrift grabbed more letters, leaving only a few in the bottom of the box.

Useless. All useless. If they said anything worth knowing, Spindrift's mother had been too lost to her obsession with the orchids to write it down in a way anyone could read. Her stomach churning, Spindrift opened the one with the neatest version of Grandfather's address, sent immediately after the last one she'd read the previous evening.

8th day of the Month of Rains, in the Year of the Ephemeral
N 33°32'0", W 7°35'0"

Dearest Papa,
I think you are the only one who will ever truly
understand.
   Love,
   Emilie

"That's it?" screamed Spindrift, balling the letter up into a wad and hurling it across the galley. "She didn't tell Grandfather anything! We'll never find it!"

There was no hope. The feeling that had grown inside of her all morning swelled like a tidal wave that threatened to sink the *Masdevallia* a second time. The blue orchid was lost, and Roland had much more time to find it. She and Max couldn't stay out here forever, away from Grandfather and Clémence.

All she wanted now was to go home to Lux. Home. It wasn't the ocean as she'd always thought. It was that city of lights and music, of hothouses and the gold- and silver-leafed trees of Magothire Street.

"Yes, she did," said Max, so quietly she almost didn't hear him. He had picked up the crumpled letter, unfolded it, and smoothed it down on the table. Now he was at the map, staring at the spot where he'd just placed a second silver pin.

CHAPTER SIXTEEN

Footsteps on the Deck

W HAT?" SPINDRIFT DEMANDED, JOINING HIM.
"Why did she go back? She wouldn't have
had time to sail back!"

"What if she didn't sail?" asked Max. "What if she
flew, or wished for some other object Monsieur Morel had
in his shop that would let her get there quickly? She'd
found half of the things he had there; she'd sent them to
him from all the ports she visited. If anyone knew what
might help her, it was her."

Spindrift pictured it, her mother on the *Masdevallia*,
waiting until everyone was asleep and wouldn't notice
her absence before taking herself to the place where she'd

hidden the blue orchid in the cave, then to a port from one of her last legible letters.

The last place she had searched for an orchid before telling Grandfather they were coming home. She hadn't found one, but perhaps she had found a safer hiding spot.

"She did tell him," Max said again. "Why send this otherwise? It doesn't say anything important. She wouldn't even have been there very long."

I think you are the only one who will ever truly under-stand. Even Grandfather had probably thought she was referring to her passion for the orchids. Emilie had sent him so many letters; by the end had he been paying any attention to where they were coming from?

Spindrift was sure he hadn't. He was so clever, so fastidious about the details of his precious objects, but this clue had escaped him.

"We'll wait until tonight," she said. Roland had to sleep, didn't he? Maybe they could get a head start before he began to follow them. "He can't spend all of his time on deck staring at us."

"Why don't we just fly there? Leave the ship so he thinks we haven't gone anywhere?"

In just the same way as Spindrift had known they had to take the *Masdevallia* to come this far, she knew they couldn't leave it now. It simply felt wrong.

"Because I'm *not* following her footsteps this time," said Spindrift.

Max put a hand on her shoulder. "Good," he said softly.

The day passed far too slowly. There were no letters left to read, the remaining ones the indecipherable puzzle pieces of Emilie's growing insanity. She paced the galley, went up to the deck, came back down again. By the time the sun began to set, she was surprised she hadn't worn a groove in her path around the *Masdevallia*.

Finally, it was dark enough to light the tallow candles. The crystal ball caught the glow of the first match strike and reflected back the wavering flame so clearly Spindrift half expected the glass to be hot when she picked it up.

"Orchid?" she called.

The orchid bloomed. "Yes, Spindrift?"

"I wish for you to take us there," she said, pointing at the two pins.

"As quickly as I can?"

"No. Just like a normal ship." If Roland did see them leave, she wanted him to wonder whether Spindrift was simply returning to Lux, heartbroken and defeated. When—if—they managed to escape sight of the *Cymbidium*, she'd hasten their course.

Slowly, the *Masdevallia* turned, and from above

Spindrift heard the snap of the sails as the wind picked up around them.

The night was even longer than the day. She and Max slept fitfully once more, counting the minutes to first light. When it finally arrived, they ran up to the deck, passing the telescope back and forth between them, scanning the horizon for any sign of another ship flying the flag of an orchid.

There was nothing. They had left the *Cymbidium* behind.

It was safer to make the next wish from below. The force of the wind as the *Masdevallia* picked up to indescribable speeds would have blown them both into the fathomless depths. Sooner than should ever have been possible, it began to slow, and through a porthole Spindrift caught the first glimpse of land, the first buildings of a beautiful, crumbling city.

If anyone in the harbor thought it strange that a ship moored itself and only two young children disembarked, they either did not say so or Spindrift couldn't understand the tongue in which they did. She didn't need to ask Orchid for help, not this time. Once on solid ground, she pulled Max through the milling crowds, searching.

Her feet stopped.

There it was.

There is a beautiful arch in the harbor here that reminds me of the ones in Lux. It wasn't exactly the same, but Spindrift could understand why her mother had said so. This one was more ornate, its outer surface etched with carvings and bright with colorful mosaics.

"Oh," said Max, understanding, but Spindrift knew he couldn't truly understand. She had told him about the signs on the arches in Lux, but he hadn't seen them for himself.

And it would be different here. Emilie had been too clever to leave the orchid on the outside of the arch, even if there were a place to do such a thing. Spindrift neared enough to touch it, ran her hands over the stone just above her head.

People stood a short distance away, watching Spindrift and muttering to one another, surely about the strange behavior of the little girl. She didn't care. Around and around the arch she went, searching.

A stone shifted under her hands.

"Help me," she said to Max, her fingernails catching painfully as she tried to grasp enough of an edge to pull. Inch by grinding inch, they worked the stone free.

She wasn't tall enough to see inside. "Here," said Max, setting the stone carefully on the ground and linking his hands together. Spindrift set her foot into them, and he hoisted her up.

There, in the hollow, was a crystal ball.

People were starting to shout now, running toward her and Max. She grabbed the orb and jumped down, staring into its center.

A time of great need. A drop of blue ink swirled within.

This one was magic itself. Would it work? "I wish for you to take us back to the *Masdevallia*!" Spindrift shouted before it could even finish blooming. They landed on the slippery deck and crashed to their knees.

Spindrift didn't know what else to do. She started to laugh, louder and louder, until the sound rang through the harbor and across the waves. She pictured the surprised expressions of the people who had witnessed their disappearance, tears streaming from her eyes. Gasping, she managed to take enough air to tell Max the joke, and he joined in, the two of them lying on the deck until their bellies ached.

It wasn't *that* funny, Spindrift knew, but relief could do that. They had found the blue orchid. Roland would never have it. When they could bring themselves to stand, they descended the stairs, and Spindrift took her black orchid from her bag. She was more used to this one. It felt . . . friendlier, somehow. She and Max braced for the turn and felt the *Masdevallia* pick up speed.

Then she wished for dinner.

. . .

"Are you all right?" asked Max.

She knew why he was asking; it didn't irritate her this time. "Yes," she said. Her mother's crazed black scribbles were still strewn across the table. Spindrift wasn't going to let herself turn into that. She felt the pull of the orchids and, with all her strength, pushed back against it.

To busy her hands, she gathered up the ruined papers and started to fold them into their envelopes—probably the wrong ones, but that hardly mattered anymore. She opened the box to see the ones inside had fallen over without the rest of them crammed in to keep everything upright. They had tipped backward, the final letter Emilie had sent resting on the top.

The address was perfectly readable, in something much closer to the neat hand in which the early letters had been written. The envelope was more creased than the others, and dirty, too, covered with grubby smudges.

She turned it over in her hands.

The paper was crinkled, as if it had been wet and then dried out again. There was no date, no coordinates.

Papa,
I haven't got much time. I can only hope this letter
finds you, and the precious cargo with it. Please,

Papa, look after her, love her as Theo and I did. That which I suspected for months now is coming to pass: Roland wants the orchids and will stop at nothing to get them. Theo is already dead, and I will be soon. I'm so sorry, Papa. I don't know what I was thinking. I wasn't thinking. I have gifted the black orchid to Spindrift; my last wish is that the boat she is in make it to shore, with that I hope she will be safe. I will have no way of knowing whether it worked, but I shall drown knowing I never should have started this quest, that it was I who brought ruin on everyone I love.

Protect her! Tell her everything one day so that she knows.

Seven Sages, what have I done?

If she survives the rain

It ended there. Spindrift shook, overwhelmed with dizziness. How long had Emilie lived after scrawling those final words? Minutes? "If I survive the rain . . . what?" she asked the air, knowing Max wouldn't have any more of an idea than she did. Had her mother wanted to tell Grandfather where the blue orchid had been all along?

"It doesn't matter," said Max, as if reading her thoughts.

He was right.

It was time go home. They'd figure out what to do with both orchids with Grandfather's help. They had stopped Roland from getting them all, and that was the important thing.

That was revenge enough.

A *thump* rang through the ship. Their heads jerked up, and they stared at each other, Max's face frozen in terror. Spindrift was sure it was a mirror of her own. She felt blindly for the orchids, grasped one with each hand, her only weapons.

Another *thump* came. Roland had boarded the ship and was coming closer.

"Get behind me," Spindrift whispered, scrambling around the table to be as far as possible from the stairs. Max pressed himself to her back, and she could feel his rapid breathing, his heartbeat pounding like a drum.

A pair of feet sounded on the top step. Spindrift could just about hear them, but she couldn't see them. Her hands gripped the orchids, and she swallowed heavily, trying to clear her throat and her head so that when the time came she could make her wishes.

She didn't know where to begin with what to wish for. All she wanted was for Roland to go away.

"Spindrift?" called a voice. Max squeaked in her ear. So sure was she that it was Roland, it took her far too long to realize that wasn't his voice. It was one she knew, one she loved.

One that shouldn't be here.

Grandfather came into view around the curve of the steps, his hands holding tightly to the railings, his face a little pale.

He didn't like ships.

Behind him, Clémence appeared, windswept and shining from the water on her skin.

Spindrift began to laugh. What a sight she and Max must look, cowering behind the table, the crystal balls in her fists as if she were about to throw them—which might not be the worst way to use them as a weapon, she thought. They were quite heavy and solid. She felt Max step away and run to hug his sister, giggles still bubbling up from her throat.

"I am old," said Grandfather, "but do I truly look that funny?"

"No," Spindrift gasped, shaking her head. She forced the rest of the hysterical laughter away and ran to him, his embrace the warmest, happiest she'd been since arriving on the *Masdevallia*.

"There, there," he said, turning Spindrift around and nudging her toward Clémence.

"You came back," said Spindrift, hugging her friend.

Clémence nodded. "Well, obviously."

"Tea, I think," said Grandfather. "That was a long, cold flight. Spindrift, can you wish it, please?"

The orchids were still in her hands. Somehow she knew without making them bloom which was which, the black one like an extension of herself. But then, in a way, that's what family was. Grandfather cleared the table just in time for a teapot to appear on it, and four china cups. She wished for lemon slices and, though he hadn't asked, cake.

They all sat down, Spindrift, Max, and Clémence all looking at Grandfather. He folded his hands around his cup and breathed in the scented steam.

"Ah, better," he said. "All right. You will know by now that I wasn't surprised to find you gone." He gave Spindrift a long stare. "A matter which you and I will return to another time. I was, however, surprised to find Clémence on my doorstep. She told me what had happened to you all up until the point where she left, and that you had found more letters. The ones I wrote to Emilie."

"I couldn't go home," interrupted Clémence. "Maman and Papa think the four of us are in Fumus, after all. Besides, Spin, I could see what was happening to you, and I hoped he could stop it. It took only a little convincing to get him to agree to come here."

"And it took only a little convincing to get her to agree

to come back with me," said Grandfather, smiling at Clémence. "How many of the letters have you read?"

"All of them," said Spindrift. "But I still don't understand everything."

"No," agreed Grandfather. "You wouldn't. Oh, don't look like that, *chérie*. You are clever enough. It is simply that those letters were between two people who didn't need to say everything because of what we already knew. Yet I see a second orchid on the table there. You managed to find a clue in Emilie's that I never did."

"But you didn't look for it," said Spindrift, sure she was right. "You hate the orchids."

Grandfather frowned into his cup and fidgeted with the cake knife before passing it to Max, who was gazing eagerly at the food. "I do not hate them," he said. "I fear them, and more important, I know I cannot be trusted to use them. What happened to your mother happened to me, too. It isn't happening to you, is it?"

"It did, a bit," said Spindrift. "At first. I think I know now how dangerous they are."

"Good," said Grandfather.

A tightness around Clémence's eyes relaxed; it wasn't until it was gone that Spindrift realized it had been there at all. She'd been so awful to Clémence. Guilt wrapped heavily around her heart.

"The orchids cost me my wife and my daughter. Everything in me wanted to hide them from you forever, and yet I knew that I couldn't. The siren call of blood is too strong. The orchids would have found you one way or another, and I thought, perhaps, there was a reason the black one came to you so young, when your mother and I were each far older. You are young enough to be thrilled by their magic but not so old that you think you no longer need me. Perhaps I simply hope that."

"No!" Spindrift jumped up and went to him, throwing herself onto his lap with such force he nearly toppled off the bench. Chuckling, he steadied them both and held her there as he'd done when she was smaller.

"I did come to the *Masdevallia* in the end," he said, "but I was too late. I watched from the shores as the last of it sank beneath the surface, taking my heart with it. I didn't yet know that Emilie had saved you before she drowned. When I discovered she had, I was so happy, Spindrift, you cannot possibly imagine."

His sweater was scratchy-soft against her cheek where she rested against his shoulder. Max cut four huge slices of cake—really, he might as well have sliced the thing into quarters—and passed them around, but Spindrift didn't touch hers. Everybody she knew and loved, her entire family both related by blood and not—

was on this ship, and still it wasn't home. Lux was home.

A sound came from up on the deck.

Everybody she knew and loved was in this galley with her.

There was only one other person it could be.

CHAPTER SEVENTEEN

Reunion

THERE, STANDING AT THE BOW, wearing his dark suit and strange smile, was Roland.

Spindrift's breath caught in her chest.

"Hello, Spindrift," he said. "Thank you for finding the final orchid for me." A crystal ball shone in each hand.

"I—I didn't!" lied Spindrift. She held the black orchid in her hand. The blue was in the pocket of her heavy cloak, hidden from sight. Max, Clémence, and Grandfather stood behind her. Roland's smile grew.

"Just as I suspected, you are not nearly so good a liar as your mother. Where is it, Spindrift?"

Something dark and defiant sparked inside of her.

"You don't get to call me that," she said. "You don't get to call me anything."

"I won't need to for long," said Roland, entirely unperturbed. "Give me the orchids and I will be on my way. Come now, Monsieur Morel, do you really wish to see your granddaughter go the way of your daughter?"

Spindrift felt Grandfather jerk with rage, but she stood fast, thinking. The orchids had driven her parents, especially her mother, to madness and death. That same feverish light still shone in Roland's eyes. If she kept the orchids that same thing might happen to her. She, too, might be reduced to a sheaf of messy black scribbles, indecipherable to anyone who tried to read her.

She wanted her normal life back, a life of dinners with Grandfather and itchy black dresses, of school and afternoons with Max and Clémence. She didn't want to spend it hunting Roland across the oceans and to the corners of the world. He was here, standing right before her in his suit marred only by the straps of a leather satchel that must be on his back.

Of course, he had the other orchids with him. He would never part from them, even for long enough to visit the *Masdevallia.* He'd need at least one, the orange one that could move people, to perform that wish anyway, and he wouldn't dare separate his collection now that he was so close. He had two, and Spindrift had two, which meant three more were in his bag.

She couldn't let him think she was surrendering too easily. His fingers began to twitch, and he bit his lips, trying to quell the obvious signs of impatience.

She couldn't make him suffer for too long, either. He'd killed her parents, sunk the *Masdevallia* once already.

"I never meant it to go so far, you know," he said. "I did not want to hurt them. Your mother tried to buy my goodwill by giving me the red one, but it was far too late for that, and I knew she would only try to get it back from me. She was obsessed, you know. Crazed. I do understand that, and so do you. You have felt the call of the orchids. You know I didn't do anything wrong. The orchids are meant to be together. Their power should never be divided."

Spindrift tried to think. The black orchid controlled objects, the blue, magic itself. But the black one was friendlier. It was hers. She turned slightly over one shoulder and then the other, nodding at Max and Clémence.

"Come and take them from me," she said, facing Roland again and reaching into her pocket so that she could hold both orchids aloft, one in each hand.

"That's right, little girl," said Roland soothingly, stepping forward. With the movement, she could see he was leaning slightly, weighted down by the other orchids on his back. "Give them to me and I will be on my way, with no reason to ever bother you or your grandfather again."

Yes, Spindrift would protect Grandfather, and Max and Clémence, too, the way Emilie had protected her in that final, all-too-brief moment of lucidity.

She looked down at her hands. The black orchid in her left, the blue in her right.

"Orchid?" she said. It bloomed, a huge, dark shadow over the deck.

"Yes, Spindrift?"

Roland's eyes gleamed brightly. He licked his lips. All he could see was the black orchid; he couldn't see Max and Clémence slowly edging around him.

"I wish for you to cut open his bag," said Spindrift.

Roland screamed with fury and spun on his toes, but that was exactly the wrong thing to do. The force of his movement sent the last three orchids flying from the neat slit in the bottom of the leather. The crystal balls rolled over the deck.

"Get them!" Spindrift shouted. Max dove to the ground, arm outstretched to catch one. Clémence got the other two.

"Monsieur Morel!" Clémence threw one of the orchids over Spindrift's head for Grandfather to catch.

"No! No, I can't!" he protested. "I shouldn't!"

"You can, Grandfather!" Spindrift said with the force of the rushing wind. "You should."

And the air was filled with wishes, an inky rainbow shrouding the deck of the *Masdevallia*. Spindrift's blue orchid stopped the magic of Roland's orange and red ones for a moment before the wish faded, weak because she didn't have the same connection to that one. Roland screamed a wish, and Max flew through the air, landing heavily against the wheel that steered the ship, but he didn't let go of his orchid. Clémence screamed and used hers to wish down a great and terrible anger as she swung her fist into Roland's face.

"Nice, Clémence!" said Spindrift.

Roland staggered, found his footing on the pitching deck. "I wish for you to kill Ludo—" began Roland softly, a deadly softness that cut through the rest of the noise.

"I wish for time to stop," said Grandfather, the first wish he'd uttered.

The world froze, ocean spray stilling in midair, the *Masdevallia* paralyzed at a slight tilt in a motionless ocean.

"It won't last long," said Grandfather. "Hurry."

Roland was still reeling from Clémence's impressive punch.

It was time. Time to put an end to this forever.

"Catch," she said.

Roland's bellow of rage carried across the water as the blue orchid flew over the railing. He dropped the orchids he held and threw himself out to catch it, his feet sliding on the slick wooden deck, his fingers closing on air as he toppled over the side of the *Masdevallia,* man and orchid both hitting the water like cannonballs.

Clémence gasped. Spindrift waited, counting, hoping. The blue orchid would sink too fast and would be almost impossible to see, clear glass in night-dark water. Even if he caught it, he would never let it go, more curse than wish. She pictured it dragging him down, down to the ocean floor, the same grave to which he had sent her parents. She strode over to the side of the ship and walked its entire length, looking down. Only when she was sure there was no sign of him did she let herself feel the enormity of what she'd done.

He'd been right. She *had* felt the call of the orchids, knew all too well what obsession with them could make a person do. Her mother had said he was charming; perhaps he once had been. The orchids had made him what he was, and made him impossible to save.

"You let it go," gasped Clémence. "They'll never be united now."

Yes, they would. But Spindrift understood what she'd done. She would have needed the power of the blue one. Her own orchid had told her once that with all of them united, nothing would be impossible.

Fame. Wealth. Power. She could have resurrected the dead.

"Grandfather," she said. He held out the green orchid, but she shook her head. "You do it."

Slowly, Grandfather walked to the edge of the ship and gazed down at the water. The green orchid fell from his hand and splashed a moment later.

"Now you, Clémence."

"Do I have to?"

"Yes," said Max, struggling to his feet. A livid bruise was forming at his temple, but he seemed steady enough. As one, he and Clémence dropped theirs. The rainbow over the ship was gone, with only the black of Spindrift's orchid left.

"I'm sorry," she said.

"Don't be," said Orchid, the last time Spindrift would hear her musical voice. "I think this is right."

Spindrift held the orb out over the water. She looked at

the crystal ball for a final time—one that couldn't show a future, but could make any future a person might imagine.

It hit the waves with a splash.

Not anymore.

She pictured it sinking, coming to rest in the same place the *Masdevallia* had slept for so long.

"Do you think your mother would mind?" asked Max. "It was the last thing she gave you."

"My mother gave it to the mist over the ocean," said Spindrift quietly. "And so did I."

Grandfather put his hand on her shoulder, and she closed her eyes, wet with the spindrift that hit her face like rain.